Blurred Faces

ALLAN RADCLIFFE

Fairlight Books

First published by Fairlight Books 2025

Fairlight Books
Summertown Pavilion, 18–24 Middle Way, Oxford,
OX2 7LG

Copyright © Allan Radcliffe 2025

The right of Allan Radcliffe to be identified as the author of this work has been asserted by Allan Radcliffe in accordance with the Copyright, Designs and Patents Act 1988.

All rights reserved. This book is copyright material and must not be copied, stored, distributed, transmitted, reproduced or otherwise made available in any form, or by any means (electronic, digital, optical, mechanical, photocopying, recording or otherwise) without the prior written permission of the publisher.

A CIP catalogue record for this book is available from the British Library.

1 2 3 4 5 6 7 8 9 10

ISBN 978-1-914148-80-4

www.fairlightbooks.com

Printed and bound in the Czech Republic

Cover Design © Hayley Warnham

Hayley Warnham has asserted her right under the Copyright, Designs and Patents Act 1988, to be identified as Illustrator of this Work.

This is a work of fiction. Names, characters, businesses, events and incidents are the products of the author's imagination. Any resemblance to actual persons, living or dead, or actual events is purely coincidental.

For Ryan and Sean
And for my dad, Bill Radcliffe

He does not hear; he will not look,
Nor yet be lured out of this book.
For, long ago, the truth to say,
He has grown up and gone away,
And it is but a child of air
That lingers in the garden there.
—'To Any Reader', Robert Louis Stevenson

Home is the place where, when you have to go there,
They have to take you in.
—'The Death of the Hired Man', Robert Frost

Jordan

David lives 1.07 miles away. I walk the blue line on the screen of my phone, the usual thrill and shame in my belly. I keep stopping to look at myself in car windows and worry at what's left of my hair.

His address turns out to be a cul-de-sac off Newhaven Road that's barely on the map.

'Jordan?'

'David?'

He's waiting on the fourth-floor landing, half submerged in darkness.

'You found the place okay, then?'

The legend across his chest reads: *Ingliston Truck and Trailer Fest 2004 – The Only Way Is Truck!* His hair's a different shape than it was in the pictures: it makes loose waves above his face. The colour seems almost blue-black until I get close and see the white asserting itself through the dark mass.

'We're in here.' He smiles, brackets appearing at either side of his mouth. 'I was half thinking of opening a bottle.'

The back of my neck ripples as I duck through the doorway. The temperature seems colder in the hallway than it was on the landing. The only burst of colour comes from the nameplate stuck to the door on my left: *RORY'S ROOM.*

He sees me looking and makes a half-arsed attempt to prise the sign off the door.

'I rented this place out to a family with a three-year-old,' he says. 'Feel like a visitor in my own home sometimes.'

The theme of austerity extends to the kitchen. The surfaces are bare. As he rootles in one of the cupboards I spy a pint glass, a couple of mugs, eggcups, a child's plastic beaker.

The red stands within easy reach. He pours himself a half tumbler then lets the bottle hover.

'I've diluting juice, tea, coffee – if you'd prefer?'

'Water's fine, thanks.'

'Right, well...'

'*Slàinte.*'

We face each other like gunslingers with our feet apart and one hand thrust down our trouser pockets. We're as butch as John Ireland and Monty Clift in *Red River*. The stance lasts just a beat too long before David yields, dropping his hip. My knee gives a twinge of relief.

'Come on, then.'

He's a man of few words, cute and shy in his vintage tee, eyes off to the side.

The bedroom that's not *RORY'S ROOM* is white and empty, with a cornice like fancy cake icing around the ceiling. I note the gunmetal-grey curtains: the smart backdrop to the selfies he posted.

His breath's fresh with the drink. I flinch but his scent isn't unpleasant. My crotch is tightening, but before we can find a satisfactory rhythm, David peels away.

'Won't be a sec.'

I stand in the middle of the floor, kneading the front of my trousers, unsure where to put myself, trying to tune out the bright sound of David peeing on the other side of the wall.

With a pang I remember I offered to cook tonight. Niall will be getting in from his work. He'll change into trackies and sit for a while at the end of the couch, thumbing through his phone with a podcast for company, or he'll do some work on Rebecca's bedroom: peeling the tape off the skirting, fitting together the chest of drawers. In about half an hour he'll start rummaging through the fridge for something edible. Luckily, my brother can make a meal out of dust and water.

I hesitate, then take off my shoes and socks, which I line up at the end of the bed. A patter of rain from outside and I see myself suddenly, a middle-aged man barefoot in a stranger's bedroom, and the absurdity of the image makes me crush my hand to my mouth to stifle a giggle.

'Here we are.'

Bare toes spark against the floorboards. Urgent now. In one movement he's tugged his T-shirt over his head and thrown it to the end of the bed. Nipples like midget gems. His body's hairless save for the ladder running down from his belly button. He slaps a palm down on his stomach and jokes that it would take him nine months to grow a beard.

I laugh too, but when I don't move, his eyes shift sideways.

'This is what you want, right?'

'Oh *yes*,' I say, with a touch too much conviction.

I lower myself onto the edge of the bed, moving with care to stop my knee from creaking. We shuffle into position, side by side. I have an urge to kiss his nose. You could hide troves in those Lee Van Cleef nostrils. He has a tattoo, I see, one of those Celtic arm bracelets: plaited strands of black. I trace its coils and ask him what it means.

'Adolescent... dumbfuckery.' He rubs at the pattern. 'Can't be undone now.'

His mouth finds mine. Cool breath: the sneaky beggar has brushed his teeth. I'm suddenly conscious of how cold my fingers are. He uses his free hand to pop open my buttons. 'Nice shirt,' he mutters, and I'm not sure if I'm meant to thank him. We both go for each other's belts at the same time, and this makes us laugh, our smiles coming together.

'Canny,' he says. 'Canny.'

We manoeuvre into place, our limbs knocking softly together, and when my knee falters, I put a hand on his chest and nudge him onto his back. He leans across to rummage for a johnny in the drawer by the bed while keeping a hold of my wrist, though whether this is to keep me in place or to stop him from falling, I'm not sure.

After the clean-up: the mortification. David eases himself off the bed and the next moment he's twirling towards the door, muttering something I can't hear. When he comes back, he's topped up his wine and he's frowning down at my refill of water.

'You taken the pledge or something?'

We hoist ourselves against the slatted board and bicker like an old couple over who gets to lay their head on whose chest. He wins and one bulky shuffle later I'm staring at the top of his head, examining the olive skin of his shoulders.

My knee. I seethe in silent agony.

He tells me about a film he saw the other night and starts running through the plot, and I tell him I know the one he means: it's a remake of an old Spanish movie. I tell him I lived in the south of Spain for a while, and he nods, pressing the edge of his glass to his lips.

'Mum was from Spain,' he says after a moment, then shrugs, so the statement floats restlessly in the air. He glances over. 'Just meant, I've never been. Not one for the heat. Hate flying.'

'Your mum was Spanish?'

'From somewhere... Galicia.'

'You speak the language?'

'Do I fuck.' He coughs. 'Sorry, *cursing*. I mean, she died when I was a kid, so I never... never any connection, know?'

He combs his fingers through his head of hair.

'You'd think I'd be used to traipsing around,' he says. 'My old boy was a field sales rep for a kitchen company. Used to cart me up and down the Highlands and the north-east, but the treat was coming back. Terra firma.'

He wriggles free, pulling his phone seemingly from nowhere, and suddenly there's music. Pedal steel guitar. Female voices. He asks if I like First Aid Kit and I hold my glass in front of my face, unsure what he means.

'This is very... nice, very easy on the ear.'

I wonder what he'd say if I told him I was into musical theatre, Eurovision, German *Schläger*.

I nod along, almost catching the beat. When I ask what he does for a living, his eyebrows lift, like I'm breaking some unwritten rule of app meets.

'I'm kind of between jobs at the moment.'

He used to manage a coffee shop called the Elbow. When I shake my head, he tells me it used to be the Square Peg Café. I'm picturing a windowed door in the New Town, tables crammed in, open sandwiches on bits of slate. I tell him I'm a teacher, and he makes the sign of the cross. He has trouble meeting my eye, which I find endearing – I'm maybe the least intimidating person I know. His is a face made of bones, the nose widening out towards gaping nostrils above a deep-coloured, full mouth.

As the silence opens out, I dredge my mind, but David gets his question in first.

'Okay, I'm just going to come out with it, and I hope you're no offended...' He stares just past me. 'What age are you... really?'

I squirm in my seat like the guilty party before admitting to forty-two. I have a year on him, he says, and my face smarts.

On the app we were both late thirties, which can mean anything upwards of the Big 4-0.

A beat then laughter, a mutual burst.

'Classic. Classic,' he says, his voice bubbling over like fizzed-up lemonade.

'You're single?'

I drop the question in like it's nothing. I don't expect it to have the effect it does. He takes a breath that seems to inflate his entire body.

'Sorry,' I say. 'Trouble with me is, I ask too many questions.'

'Sure, I'm single.'

He smiles, but it's a forced smile, his expression stiffening. I wonder again at the near-empty flat, the sadly depleted cupboards. The only ornament in this room is one of those balls made of coloured elastic bands, perched on the chest of drawers.

David arches his back against the mattress.

'No one in your life?' He clears his throat, feigning disinterest. 'No one, know…?'

And of course, I picture Lev, his smile fading as he took in everything I had to say to him that night in the Thai restaurant. My big speech: I had practised until it was second nature, pacing my flat, trying out all my faces in the mirror. When I saw it wasn't going the way I wanted I started blethering, all the while longing for a fire alarm to intervene. Lev's English was imperfect, but his response came at me like the honed point of an arrow.

'Jordan, I think there has been a misunderstanding.'

He was sitting across from me, half of a spring roll hovering in chopsticks, suspended between plate and waiting mouth. I stared down at my place setting: at the tumbleweed of shredded vegetables and beansprouts, the inevitable rose carved out of carrots. I tried to find something to say that wouldn't sound bitter or bitchy.

'Nah. There's no one,' I say now.

'Couple of single guys.'

'Right.'

'Right.'

'Well. My turn for *el baño*.'

Standing peeing in the bathroom, I spot the soap bag stationed on top of the cistern, unzipped, stuffed to the gunnels. A single towel slung over the edge of the bath. I take a peek into the living room. It looks as though it's only occupied for watching television or playing music, which I assume is accessed from the breezeblock by the window. There are records, DVDs and paperbacks spilling out of an upended Bag for Life. The whole set-up feels temporary. I've a notion to get down and shuffle everything into stacks.

Lev once told me I had a touch of the OCDs. He made it sound like an affliction you could cure with a cream from Boots. He used to end himself at the sight of me wiping down the tables in the college canteen with Handy Andies.

Dressed, I hover with my hands clasped, more self-conscious somehow with my clothes on than when we were fully naked.

'You know,' he says, 'if you pull yourself into that corner and tilt your noggin a full ninety degrees, on a sunny day you can see one edge of the castle.'

'Ah...' I take a step back, pulling the curtain, braced for the feeling of melancholy the Edinburgh skyline always awakens in me, but of course all I can make out is my own reflection against the dark. Behind me, David has pulled the covers up to his chest. He's leaning forward, his eyes fixed, as though taking me in for the first time.

'You were at the High, weren't you?'

In the moment after he asks, I wonder if I should just lie. As I turn from the window, readying my smile, his face comes back into focus, tight and alert.

'Yeah. Yeah, I was.'

'Knew I knew you from somewhere. You're Jordan Grieve.'

Of all the gin joints in all the world...

'You just fell into place.' He thumbs his chest. 'I was David Lockin. Year below. We had a couple of classes together. Art. Biology. Third and fourth year. Mrs Petrie.'

'Petri Dish? There was a horror story.'

'You don't remember me?'

I look at his face, trying to remould it, make it take on a younger shape, but I can't find anything of our shared past in all those jutting bones.

'Sat two benches behind you. Spent two years staring at your back. Not surprised you don't remember. I was a ghost back then. Didn't lift my head till I was seventeen.'

'Your face,' I say, as though saying it will make him more familiar.

'I mind *you*,' he says, 'because you had a brother, right? Few years ahead?'

'Niall.'

'He was... cute.'

My brother, with his permanent mantle of cigarette smoke and fondness for cracking his neck every other minute.

'Oh, he's in life assurance now. St Andrew Square.' It's the sum total of my knowledge of what Niall does with his days, but it elicits another nod of recognition.

'Your mum was a nurse. She was on the ward my auntie was in for her dementia.'

'The old High's gone now,' I say, before he gets nostalgic for my dad, and his habit of turning up still toasted from the night before to rewire people's houses.

'Aye, they flattened it and built a new one.'

David drags the covers up over his chest, which I take as a sign for me to go. But my mouth keeps talking in spite of myself, filling the air with place names and names of teachers and kids whose faces have gone blank with time, some of whom he remembers and others not, and all this blather because I don't have the effrontery to ask David why he's between jobs and why he's living on this kiss curl of a street in a flat with nothing but an elastic band ball to show for his forty-odd years, and whether or not he wants to meet again, before I leave.

'It's all quite a long time ago.'

He nods, keeping count of the years. My knee's starting to tell from all this standing. David's glass sits idle on the floor. He looks away. A kind of adolescent shyness has crept between us. It was the mention of school that did it. Passion killer.

The only way to keep the silence at bay is to dig out our phones and go through the panto of swapping numbers.

'Yeah, let's keep in touch,' he says, his voice a thin line, as he punches at the screen. 'I'm not looking for a relationship or anything.'

'Me neither.'

He at least has the good grace to look up from his phone.

I don't bother telling him that I'll be leaving town in a few days' time.

He comes to show me out, wearing the duvet. The thought of that corkscrew body under the shapeless layer makes me hover. For all his seeming hurry to get me out into the night, the kiss he gives is loose-lipped and sincere.

Outside, the rain has thinned. It's still and cool, the best kind of evening for a run. I lean my weight onto my knee, lowering slowly, all the while looking up at what I think is his bedroom window. David Lockin. I try again to make him twenty years younger in my head, but the picture won't come; even the up-to-date version is starting to blur. But I can still feel him in the bits of me he put his mouth on. My knee grinds as I straighten my leg. I need to get better. I have to get moving. This is the bit of the meet I don't like: the hangover, the little death. So I put him behind me. I turn towards Ferry Road and the prospect of another night folded up on Niall's couch. I hope he's left some of whatever he's made for dinner. I'm starved.

Davie

Door clicks and the silence rings, louder than before. Jordan Grieve. Fuck me. With the quilt still round me I go from room to room, turning on lights. Firing up the tunes. Into the shower for a quick dook and then I grab up my glass and sit scuddy with my feet pulled under me. For a good fifteen seconds I manage a half-decent impersonation of one of those happy loners.

Here's where I grew up. The old boy and I used to sit and size each other up from opposite ends of this room. I can still see him slumped in his chair, puggled from work. He signed the place over to me when he and Lucille left, saying it was an asset, something to make up for the pension I didn't have and probably never would have. Something of my own that was separate from Frank. He was sometimes on the money, that faither of mine.

I was kidding myself on when I came back. Thought I might find something in the place that would reboot me. There's fuck all left of my childhood except that reek of old fags at the back of the hall cupboard. I try to imagine what this room would look like if I went and got the rest of my shit from Frank's, but I find I can't. Mind's a blank.

Now I've got Christine and the Queens in one ear and the blare from the neighbour's TV in the other. I won't stay long. I'll get up in five and pull on my jacket, still damp from the day, and take to the pavement like I did yesterday and the day before, head down, one step after another, lasting out as long as I can before the pull gets too strong and I end up back on his street that used to be our street, hoping for a look or a sign.

Jordan Grieve, though. His wee coupon. Oblivious.

Regent. There'll be friendly faces in the Regent.

There'll be faces.

Dead tonight. A man resting his belly on the bar lifts a hand. Two silver heads turn from the television and nod in my direction.

This barman's new on me. 'How're you going?' Nice teeth with a gap the size of a terraced house in the middle. 'Mind me? Greg? I know your, uh… I'm a friend of Frank's.' Then, all quiet: 'Here, I'll do my staff discount – Frank's a good pal.'

He puts my voddy in front of me, and I try to find some words, but he just gives a nod and retreats to the other end of the bar.

Nine-oh-four says the clock above the taps. I squire my voddy into the corner with the best views. Red walls, tartan carpet, shiny green seats: décor's been the same in all the years I've been coming here. Where the white of the flat makes me cold all over, this place is a home from home.

The two old guys under the telly have spun around in their seats. They sit with their heads together. One of them whispers in his pal's ear and the pal looks over with his wet eyes. More of Frank's pals. Auld Reekie's branch of the Friends of Dorothy. They should all have to wear a wee badge or something.

Aye, it's me, I want to shout over. David's the name. Davie to my pals. Vodka and who-cares-if-you're-buying? When I return their looks, they shrivel away, swivelling back to their snooker, kidding on they've not been nosying.

Nine twenty-eight. Boy comes through the doors – my age, ginger. One of those Captain Birdseye beards to compensate for the lack of anything up top. I try out a smile. But he disappears around the curve of the bar, pulling back his arm to bump fists with the lovely barman.

Nine fifty-four. Barman sees me heading over and lines up my next one. Melon Belly's gazing at the drips running down the side of his pint glass. As I retake my pew, I'm once again conscious of the empty place across from me.

Not that I'm lonely, mind. More... exposed. Like one of those dreams where you're bum-naked in an exam.

I go for my phone, and there's Carol checking in. *How's tricks?* Good old Carol. I lift my drink, readying my reply, and at that exact moment Jordan comes back to me.

Jordan Grieve. He was almost out the door before it clicked who the hell he was. Fresh face, freckles, round blue eyes. At first, he seemed such a stiff in his very nice jacket and chinos, thank you very much: everything smart and sober like he'd taken a wrong turn on his way to the Lyceum.

It was when he was standing at the end of the bed that he turned into fifteen-year-old him again: a bit glaikit, off in his own head. Teeth untidy when he smiled, same as I remember. Poor guy. Always a big chunk of fruit. Something wholesome about him, something sweet, and they hurt him for it.

I mean, *we* hurt him.

We hurt him.

Me and Hutton and the rest of them.

Should've asked him to stay. He might have come to the pub. We might have swapped stories. That smile was a tonic. All the weight of him seemed to be in that stretch of the mouth. A few voddies in and I might have fessed up, reminded him who I was. What we did.

I might have said my sorries.

'OH, WOULD YOU LOOK AT THAT,' shouts one of the olds as the underdog sneaks another frame.

Ten twenty-seven. Chucking out time soon, and then what? *Then what?*

Frank. Nothing else for it. Cash in one of my tokens. It's been a fortnight. My shit's gathering dust at the house. We're supposed to be – what did he say? – *uncoupling*. Meant as a joke but excuse me for not laughing. More than once in the past few days my thumb's floated over his number. I've deleted a few texts, not wanting to be first to crack.

'Davie?'

At first, he sounds not all there, like I'm dragging him away from something. When I tell him in as chipper a voice as I can manage that I'm thinking of dropping by, there's nothing but dead air.

'David, it's nearly eleven.'

'I was thinking we could catch up, like.'

'Should I be worried?'

'We could maybe watch something on the box.' (We were halfway through *Queer Eye* series two when I finally departed, and there's a million episodes of that shit.) 'Just an hour, before bed.'

'Are you... have you been drinking? Okay, I'm coming. I'll come and pick you up.'

Pricked by his concern I move the phone closer to my mouth. Tell him to stay put.

'I'm not even pished,' I say, like a wean.

Another silence, and then: 'Okay. Come on, then.'

I leave my vodka. The door clangs behind me, cutting off the barman's 'Mind how you go,' and I head down the way towards London Road. Haven't been walking two minutes before the rain starts again. It's not heavy, just a ball ache.

Sometimes I actually fucking hate Scotland.

*

This house that used to be my home is one quarter of this great thug of a villa up the Willowbrae. He opens the door, peering out slowly, like he's expecting a bunch of hingers-on from the pub. He looks at me top to toe, taking in my soaked hair, the limp sleeves. An edge to his smile. For a moment I think he's going to send me away, like the kid that used to go round selling tablet: *None today, thanks!*

In the kitchen he chucks me a towel and starts on the kettle. Once I've rubbed my face and hair dry, I stay in the doorway, looking over at the stack of paper lined up along the table-edge.

'What you working at?'

'Oh, you know, it's that woman who wrote that thing about holidaying in war zones. She's got a podcast. I'm interviewing her tomorrow morning at half ten.'

'Between war zones, is she?'

'She's a schoolteacher who travels in her holidays. I might pitch it as the hook for a feature about travel books for Christmas. Or something. It's quite a *compelling* story.'

I smile into myself as I take the mug from him. *Compelling, vibrant, innovative* – all the guff that comes up again and again in his writing. Frank bingo. Whatever dislike or anger he feels towards his work he keeps well-hidden. After firing off his latest article, he'll open a fresh document, key in the subject and off he goes again: hands thumping the keys, face set. In the zone.

He shoves a plate of toast on the table. Four doorsteps between us. Thinks I need feeding up. I've got a notion for one of those wee cans he keeps in the fridge for emergencies. M&S gin and tonic, sweet like cough mixture, only I don't like to presume since we're *uncoupling*. Sink into my chair as he flicks on the speakers at the edge of the worktop, and the first chords of that song 'There's No Time Like the Future' creep their way into the room. Song's a slow, bass-driven thing, about someone crushing on someone who doesn't even know he exists. Frank loves it, but I think there's something stalkerish about the whole thing. I forget the singer's name.

Frank lifts the heelie of the bread. Finds his red pen. It's only when he comes towards the light that I see his hair's changed. It's cut in a straight line across his forehead, still wavy at the back and shaved at the sides. Kind of a mullet type thing. I've never seen him like this. He was shaggy the whole time we were together.

'Let me just get through this bit – I won't be a minute.'

He's always been a big eater: some kind of reaction against the rationing of his childhood in a big fuck-off West Coast family. Never leaves a crumb. As he chews on his toast, he lowers his head to his notes, scooping out the important bits with his sharp eye. He doesn't mind me sitting here like a big dope. Holding the mug gives me something to do with my hands.

I love this room, with everything just so: the floorboards, the old sideboard, the coffee machine, the fair-trade wooden fruit bowl, that framed print of waves turning into rabbits. My idea of home, but I don't say that to him.

His ancient iPod ticks onto the next track. Guitar strokes settling into a brisk rhythm. A light male voice: *You never even tried...*

'We went to see him live, no?' I say.

'That was you and Luca, wasn't it?'

In this flat, Frank's music plays all the time. Always the same sad stuff, which is maybe weird for someone who's been in and out of the doldrums.

In the summer, between shifts, hanging around the flat like stoor, I could hear his sounds behind the door to the study as he worked. Chet Baker, Ella Fitzgerald, Nina Simone, all the singer-songwriters he loved.

Then I catch you smiling –

Was it something I said?

Or something I can't see, locked up inside your head?

'Don't you ever get fed up listening to that stuff?'

'Course not,' he says, with a sigh. But he turns a moment later and reaches for the dial just the same.

When we were first together, back in prehistory, he was still working for the rag that had taken him on as a trainee, taught him the difference between a story and a waste of paper. He stood apart from the ones that spent their lunchtimes in the pub. Flew up through the ranks. But he got fed up doorstepping grieving mothers and sitting through trials at the Sheriff Court, seeing the same poor souls bob up in the dock. For a while the freelance life seemed to suit him. For a while.

He gets up now, lifting the plate. I've managed half a slice. He grabs the other half, folds it up and down it goes. Bottomless pit. As I'm watching, my thoughts rewind to Jordan. The way he seemed to be shooting bolts of life out his eyes, leaning with interest towards everything I was saying.

'You remember...' I say to Frank. 'You mind I told you my mum was from Spain?'

'Yeah.' He leans against the counter. 'Rings a bell. Why?'

'No reason.'

I can't remember us ever talking about her. Not in any real way. In all those years, I don't think she was ever mentioned in this flat.

'Her name was Paula, by the way.'

'What's that?'

'Doesnae matter.'

Behind me he's pulling the door to the dishwasher.

'You're feeding yourself?'

'Course.'

'Have you been back to work?'

'Not... yet.'

'Davie.'

I tried. I tried. I went back to grinding fresh-roasted beans and putting hearts on the tops of lattes for a couple of weeks, but, well, my heart wasn't in it.

'I'm on a career break.'

'Is that so?'

Frank, behind me, hovering.

'How's the flat?'

'Same as ever.'

I focus on the pattern of the table cover, which is all sunshine and pineapples, and not in any way appropriate for the season. I'm wondering if I can just say nothing and hope he leaves me be. Wish I could shrink myself down to Thumbelina size and just make a bed for the night in my mug.

No idea how I managed to cling on here long as I did. Seems kind of pathetic now. For a while, my tenants were my excuse. *Oh, I need to give them notice. Oh, the flat's needing a lick of paint.* I'd start taking my stuff across in dribs and drabs, then get the absolute horrors and not finish. 'Is your flat still not ready?' Frank wanted to know, and course I'd get all touchy and lie that it was in progress.

My goodbye happened almost without either of us noticing. I mean, it just *happened*. One night, instead of going to the spare room after *Scotland Tonight*, I kissed him on the head in what I thought was a final way. Then I just walked out the front door. Hadn't known I'd do it till it was done.

All the way across town I had the total fear. Terrified, like a kid running away from home. By the time I got to the flat he'd texted.

Where are you?

Three days later, there was another text – *Missing you* – and when I went back there was wine, and we got so pished together that I ended up staying.

'You don't mind me being here?' I said afterwards.

'I'm glad you're here,' he said. And then he put his arm across and held on for what felt like half the night.

'Let's try not to do this tomorrow,' he said, and I didn't know if he was serious or not.

We shift through. He sits with his chair pulled close to the box, so he doesn't have to strain his eyes. We're watching the day's news, Starmer and Reeves humping around in hard hats, and Frank's got the sound nearly on mute with the subtitles stumbling across the bottom half of the screen. One talking head after another, each of them allowed their tuppence worth. Leaves me punch-drunk. Frank was a Starmer fan, and now he's pissed off the world didn't suddenly get better. That's why he's got bugged-out eyes, searching the screen for some bright sign.

He sighs and turns over to *Family Guy*. It's 'Road to Rhode Island', an episode we've seen about a million times.

This is nice. This is what I'm talking about.

On the other side of the room the hand holding his glass goes up and down, smooth as an appliance. Here we are, each other's family in a way. His folks are long gone. The old boy and me, well, that's what it is. Frank's brothers and sister are all round the globe: New Zealand, Japan, somewhere down south. At his mum's funeral his siblings were as tongue-tied around him as they were with me.

Steven, who worked at one of his old papers, was Frank's only other long-term squeeze, far as I know. Their hobbies were eating in nice restaurants and travelling. And they both worked long hours, and stayed together for a few years, until the whole thing just fizzled out. I could never picture them together. Steve had hair like candyfloss, no kidding, texture *and* colour. I'd been told the flat they shared had a line running down the middle of the study, with Steve's explosion on one side and Frank's G-Plan on the other.

Frank used to say he knew I was his one true love when he realised he didn't care about my lax standards.

'Davie...'

He's looking across, his face appalled.

'Fuck. Sorry.'

Tears filling my eyes so I can't see.

I hear his chair scraping the floorboards and next thing he's putting an arm around me, and I'm ugly-crying worse than ever.

'Where'd that come from?'

A rush in my ears.

'Hooft, I'm not quite... there yet, you know?'

'We made this decision together, remember?'

Tip my head back, try to snort it all back in. *Greetin Teenie*. My dad's name for me. *Pull yourself together, son*.

'It was a mutual decision, Davie,' says Frank, and I hear him sigh.

Somewhere, in the near distance, the whirl of a police siren. Kids in the park shouting the odds.

'David, when was the last time you slept?'

From nowhere a yawn splits my head in half.

'Look, you can stay here tonight. The spare room's all made up.'

Uncoupling. We're supposed to be uncoupling.

But the thought of that room and the big, massive bed is making my limbs heavy.

Wipe away my tears and snotters.

'You've still got your key, have you?'

Part of me wants to keep him here, just talking about nothing, but I'm too tired to make any kind of sense and he's antsy, the way he's drumming his fingers against the arm of the couch. Wanting his own bed, then up early for tomorrow's interview with that teacher who goes her holidays in war zones.

That's fine. There's tonight. Tonight, I'll sleep.

*

Down to my boxers. Sheets smell of that sickly fabric stuff he insists on using.

Curl up with my phone so I can text Carol.

Back at F's. Will call tomorrow.

Switch off quickly to avoid the roasting that's coming my way.

I turn onto my side and brace my mind against sore thoughts. Only sound that comes is Frank sighing to himself as he pads to the bathroom. I arrange myself against the pillows, not sure what I want, whether I've even got the energy for him.

The soft click of his bedroom door.

Last time I was here, somewhere in the night, the door opened, and in he came. Without a word he lifted the covers and dropped in beside me, like I'd never left, and I let myself sink against him. In the early morning he went away, and then we acted like it hadn't happened.

Some nights I dream he's in bed beside me. I'll reach over from my side and, finding nothing, I'll remember, and it's like a spasm racks my whole body.

Lying there, trying to make myself float, I think of Jordan again.

He was losing his hair, receding in a nice way. Feels a lifetime ago that I opened the door to him. His aftershave stayed in the air after he left.

Jordan Grieve. All grown-up, a bit of a bobby-dazzler.

Thank fuck he didn't recognise us.

Not that I ever put the boot in, never that. Least, not that I remember. But I was there, I was a part of it. Ringside seat. Laughing while they did what they did.

The memory of his round face is kind of soothing, like those photos of holiday places that bob up when the computer screen goes quiet.

His number's in my phone. If I feel like it, I can get in touch. If I want to see him again, I know where to find him.

Like I'd ever actually text him!

I turn on my side for a while, pretending to be a different person. Bold. Wondering what the hell I'd say to him, how I'd put it.

Hi Jordan, it was great to meet up with you again...

Nice to see you the other day, Jordan...

Lovely to bump into you again...

Are you maybe free sometime to...?

If you're free sometime maybe we could...?

Maybe, if you're free...?

The word repeats in my head over and over as sleep pulls me down.

Maybe

Maybe

Maybe

Jordan

Bap-bap-bap on the other side of the wall. *Bap-bap-bap-bap-bap.* When eventually I've disentangled myself from the blankets and cushions and shambled through, the hammering has ceased, and my brother is kneeling in a circle of cardboard and cellophane. The frame of a child's bed gleams out of the debris.

'Come see,' he says.

He places a hand on the box spring and leans against it, nodding over my shoulder. I turn and confront a green wall and a yellow plastic light in the shape of a crescent moon that's rising from carpet to ceiling. It's like being dunked inside a cartoon.

'When are you expecting her?'

'Saturday, all being well.' He passes a hand over his head. 'You'll still be here on Saturday? Okay. Good. She'll want to see you.'

With effort, I creak to my knees, and together we lift the bits of plastic and cardboard, scooping the spare screws.

'I thought I'd go up and see Mum tomorrow.'

'Thursday's the Nursing Fellowship. Jordan, you can't just *drop in* and see our mother. Arrangements must be made in advance. The calendar has to be consulted.'

'You seen her lately? Mum?'

'We talk on the phone every night. Lately, when she's called, we've mostly talked about Rebecca.'

He shoots another look at the feature wall.

'Think she'll like all this? The bairn?'

We face the crescent moon, our heads on one side. Rebecca's almost nine now. When I think of her, I see a child of four, clarty hands from playing out, the little group of friends piling through the back door at Niall and Claire's house in Queensferry. A solemn face: when she smiled you knew she meant it.

'Are you absolutely sure she likes green?'

His mouth twitches, he spits a laugh. Then he coughs and looks away, mortified at his lack of restraint.

'Aye, she likes green, so I'm told.'

Niall suggests a bite at the new place on the corner of Bernard Street. I pull on my brightest knit and my brother presses his lips because he thinks it's safer for me to be in full mourning when I'm home. We step out into a monochrome day. Since splitting up with Claire, Niall has been staying in a flat near the shore, about as far north as you can get without falling in the Forth. Every available edifice has been hollowed out and remade so the disposable income brigade can enjoy a glimpse of the Fife coastline with their nine-pound glass of wine.

We perch on swivel stools and order the full Scottish. When I clarify that I want the veggie option, Niall stares but says nothing. I can't tell him I've got Lev's ghost on my shoulder, hectoring me about how bad the meat industry is for the planet.

The counter guy brings a pot of coffee and orange juice in jam jars with straws. I watch my brother fish out the stripy tube and break the surface of his drink with his lips, making a face like he knows it's good for him.

'How long's it been, Niall?'

'Six months, near enough. One hundred and seventy-nine days, if you're interested.'

'This is the longest...?'

He shrugs.

'You're doing well on it. I mean: you've got a bit of colour in your cheeks.'

A round of coughing as he signals the waiter, waving his jar.

'More of this... *stuff*, please.'

The story goes that when our father first held Niall in his arms he peered down and said, 'He's giving me a dirty look, the boy.'

I'd say it was meant to be funny, a bit of bravado to hide his terror at the thought of taking a real live baby home.

Niall and Peter: the pair of them seemed always to circle each other. Even the things they did together didn't require anything in the way of verbal communication.

They watched the Hibs with their feet on separate bits of the furniture. On holidays they punted a ball back and forth while looking just past each other or they played snooker, whistling at each other's shots.

I don't remember my brother ever calling him Dad. Mum was always Mum, never Jenny or Jen. Dad was always Peter: the nuisance lodger. A fly to be swatted aside when he buzzed between Niall and our mother.

But I'm told that almost as soon as I was able, I would hold up my hand whenever Dad came into the room. *Here I am, I'm yours.* We knew each other inside out and he tried to bring me up with every bit of himself.

This is how I choose to remember it.

He was the go-to electrician for the neighbourhood. Saturday mornings, I'd walk round Clermiston and Drumbrae with him and sit eating Babybels while he climbed ladders and felt around for wires and fittings before sewing everything up again and collecting his tools.

He would take things apart – plugs, pieces of fruit, flowers – to show me what they were made of. Once, my mum came back to find the house deserted and his bag abandoned on the living room floor. The front door was unlocked; it might even have been left open. We had taken the bus to the airport because I had never seen a plane take off.

'How's the wee one getting on?' people would ask Mum.

'Ask his father,' was always her answer. 'Thick as thieves, those two.'

Niall raises his jam jar.

'Anyway, so here's to you. Been a while.'

'You'll need to come down. You and Rebecca.'

'Long time since I was in London, right enough.'

'In the new year, then, once you're in a routine with her.'

'That's a done deal.'

In the past two decades I've lived in Spain, France, the Czech Republic and Stoke Newington. My brother hasn't visited me in any of them. I wouldn't even bet on him owning a passport.

When I phoned and told him I was thinking of coming home for a few days in November he asked if something was the matter. 'Nothing's happened?'

'Do I need an excuse to see my one and only brother?'

I could hear his breath juddering on the line.

'Well,' he said, 'it's been – what – five years?'

The food arrives and we eat diligently, not really speaking. I blear out the window. The sun has come out with a sudden intoxicating heat. Everyone that goes past carries that look of steaming relief that comes with a gap in the clouds.

Five years is a long time. Even allowing for the pandemic, the unimpeachable excuse of being locked down in a corner of a foreign country, I could have made a point of visiting earlier. Now I feel like I'm sitting with an acquaintance, like I can't curse or spill in front of him. The radio behind the counter is playing 'One Day More' from *Les Mis* and I have to swallow over my desire to join in. Niall's hunched over his plate and he's pushing forkfuls into his mouth. I imagine timidly offering him a crash course in Grice's conversational maxims, one of the few remembered nuggets from my English Language degree.

Drunk Niall's so much easier. Drunk Niall is an open book. I have always had to guess what Sober Niall is thinking. There are times when I have to ask him open questions, the way I would the more challenging of my students, to elicit answers of more than one syllable.

I love him, but I'm not sure if he likes me. I mean, I know that Drunk Niall loves me, because he's told me often enough.

Sober Niall, well, that's a whole other mystery.

The devil in me wants to start telling him I had it off with an old classmate last night, just to see how he reacts.

Niall and Jordan. Our teachers had field days. *Did your mum and dad have a thing about rivers?* The truth was less poetic. Niall was named after a friend of our dad from his roaring days. Mum had her heart set on Jordan for me: boy or girl. They didn't clock what they'd done until it was too late. Dad thought the whole thing hilarious. Mum worried the neighbours would think they were hippies.

In our family lore, everything was either 'a Niall thing' or 'a Jordan thing'. He loved numbers, stats, facts. I preferred stories, listening to my Walkman, hearing our mother play the piano. He was the sociable one, with the friends at the door, while I was off in my head or glued to the television. But we ended up looking alike, with our mother's height and our dad's colouring. Scottish blue, Dad called it, like a breed of cheese.

Ur yeez twins? was a line we heard a lot.

I admired him, Niall, his easy smile and quiet strength. I was in thrall to the Sunday paper round he could do in fifteen minutes on his bike. Soon he would graduate to the Wimpy on Princes Street where all the best-looking girls in his year worked. I inherited the paper round, and made a hash, the final straw coming when I trampled down someone's newly laid cement pathway while deep in the *Chess* soundtrack. A phone call was made. My fate was sealed before I'd returned to the paper shop.

We spent our summers in caravan parks and campsites where he made pals in the swing park or by the pool, and I was allowed to tag along.

Despite the resemblance, where he was lean, I was a string bean. Least little thing and I was in tears. Niall was never the clingy, frightened type. He seemed the one set to pull himself through his own life.

But it was Niall who stayed and me who went away.

He drops his fork.

'Well, if that was my lunch, I've had it.'

He reaches behind him and feels in his coat pocket, bringing out a pouch of tobacco and some fag papers in a fluster of coins and paper hankies.

I watch him fumblingly fashion a roll-up.

'You still jogging and that?'

'I'm resting. I've done something to my knee.'

'Getting old.'

'It's just a twinge.'

I'd been weaving along the pavement in Stoke Newington when someone hanging out of a van shouted *Get your knees up, mate!* Of course, I had spun around, the better to put a pretty face to the voice (the driver was nothing to look at), and as I turned back, I slipped off the kerb, landing strangely. When I'd recovered my dignity I could barely straighten my left leg. Rubbernecking will be the death of me.

'Running's not good for you,' Niall says. 'Not at your age.'

He smiles, the glint coming into his eyes.

Lovely.

'Niall, you remember a guy called David Lockin? Year below me.'

'Trouble?'

'How do you mean?'

'He went to the jail. Cracked somebody's skull.'

'Oh, now that's Aiden Culver you're thinking of. Lockin. It's quite a… an unusual name. Wee guy. Quite a… slim face. Dark, thick hair. I kind of… caught up with him last night. He remembered everything about us. He mentioned Mum. He remembered you.'

I stop shy of telling my brother that David called him cute.

'Funny, isn't it, that he should have remembered all that?'

'I quite often think about when we were kids,' Niall says. 'More than ever these past couple of years.'

He takes a slurp, the packet of ciggie papers poised between his fingers. It has taken a while for me to notice the change in his personal smell, the absence of underlying sharpness. Despite his years of imbibing, he has never acquired a gut. His profile is as sharp at forty-seven as it was at twenty-four.

I can barely remember a time when Niall and Claire weren't together. They met in the Conan Doyle one Saturday when Claire was over to see a gig at the Playhouse. When they were first an item, they were allowed to spend weekends in our flat. Claire's mum and dad were old-school religious and wouldn't let Niall stay over, not even in the spare room.

Saturday nights, when they were skint, I'd sit with them while they watched *Blind Date*, *Casualty*, *Stars in Their Eyes*. I liked Claire: she had time for me. *Wee bro*, she called me. Our chatter would drop off after a while and the place would fall silent save the rattle from the telly, and after a while the nose-breathing would start up from the other end of the couch, and it would intensify.

A feeling came to me off the faux leather, something I couldn't name, collecting in the air and wafting towards me. Excitement and sadness, both. Just when I was getting ready to scuttle away, Niall and Claire would rise with contented sighs and edge towards the door – 'Night then, Jordan,' – bound for the double mattress wedged between the walls of the box room. Not very private, but it was more comfortable than the graves in the Eastern Cemetery.

'I'll get the bill.'

His face becomes tense as he strains in his seat, attempting to signal to the counter guy, who's leaning over, talking to another customer.

'God's sake, do his lips never get frayed...'

He returns to his roll-up, letting his mouth hang open, tightening the skin around the tobacco with one hand while agitating his stubble with the other. He looks up and tries out his grin, half-heartedly, a poor impression of his most charming self.

I have always thought of him as our mother's son, but in that moment I see our father and I have to look away.

Dad. Peter. Pete. He was more than one person, of course he was. He was well liked. He couldn't settle. He'd walk into a room unnoticed and leave four hours later everyone's bestie.

You'd see him at the start of a gathering, getting an instinct. If there were people he didn't know he'd cling to my mother or someone he knew, making a start on his lager. He'd grow into the room, turning the conversations, making connections. And there were no half-measures with my dad. If he liked you, he really liked you.

He always spoke to me on equal terms, as though I had arrived in the world a grown adult. Come to think of it, he never talked down to anyone, never condescended. He used the same gentle tone with me that he used with my mother, with his friends.

He seemed to think I was born objective about everything. I never once heard him raise his voice.

His decline came slowly; it gathered around us. When he stopped working, we moved into a flat on the fifth floor of an eight-storey Lego-brick block on the Southside. The development was so new that the clutter from the site hadn't been cleared away: it lay in heaps around the building for what felt like years.

All of the baby-fat freshness was gone from him. I couldn't look anymore. I went hunting for his stashes. I got together his bottles in a bag but then I just stood there, in the middle of the kitchen: my plan wasn't fully formed.

Niall, watching from a corner of the room, suddenly came to life.

'I know what to do.'

We stepped out into the landing. The rubbish chute was in one corner, behind a heavy swing door. It had fascinated us when we moved in: we hunted for things we could throw in it, the noisier the better.

Niall and I squeezed through the door with the clanking bag. We took it in turns to push the bottles through the narrow opening. Niall drove them down the chute with such force it made me flinch.

He was seventeen or eighteen then, in his final year at school. There was an edge to him, a kind of aggression. He was at times a good brother to have around. In the rammy of high school he stayed close, helicoptering in when he saw that I was in difficulty. He had this quiet authority. He could scatter a crowd with a look – or so it seemed.

Niall and I head back along the road, our breath stealing a march on us.

'It's just so bastard dark already,' he says, a kind of awe in his voice.

We both spy a Christmas tree posed in a second-floor window, and its effect is telling; I say *ooooooh*, pointing, while he physically recoils.

I try to make him laugh by cavorting along the pavement. *Step on the cracks and the bears will get you.*

Up in the flat, my brother gives me a vague instruction to help him straighten the place while he lugs the hoover through to Rebecca's bedroom. My holdall is arranged at one end of the couch, the arm of my pink Séfr shirt lolling down the side. This is all I've got with me, one measly bag, the layers of clothes interspersed with sheets of Bounce, but when I had packed for the trip my flat looked almost as empty as when I moved in.

Just before Reading Week, Lev packed up the books and DVDs and CDs I'd lent him and left the box sitting on my desk in the English department nook. A card inside: *Thanks for all of these things. I enjoyed all of them. See you when you get back from vacations, I always look forward to talking to you.* A reminder of his number at the end.

Sitting there, sifting through the neat pile, I felt myself slump. He'd packed everything in a shoebox. I had been preparing myself for a silence from him, averted eyes in the corridor. This was so much better and kinder, so like Lev, and so much harder to take.

I met him at a party. Ruth, a colleague from the English department had invited all of us round to celebrate her fiftieth. Weeks in advance, she went round the staff room, handing out invitations enclosed with self-drawn maps showing the location of her flat.

She answered my knock, already tipsy. 'Here we are,' she said, barely aware of who I was, whirling me towards the kitchen. Lev was at the other end of the room. He had a bottle in one hand, which he waved in the air as he talked. He was part of a group of three or four who formed a semicircle around him.

Blurred Faces

I knew his face. He'd started at the college around half term. He was young, mid-twenties, and he had smartly combed hair and unabashedly thick eyebrows. He wore a shirt and a jacket every day when most of the students were in jumpers and jeans at best and he was always with at least one other person, leaning or directing his gaze. He wasn't my student, but I knew from the way the other teachers spoke about him that he was diligent, well-liked, a favourite.

I unloaded the bags of Revels and crisps I'd brought onto the table, glancing over a couple of times. His voice surprised me. The tone was lighter than I'd expected, with the elongated e, like an Italian speaker.

Just as I was contemplating squeezing past the little group and trying my luck in another room, Lev turned, holding out a hand, which had the effect of yanking me a couple of steps forward on an invisible leash.

'Excuse me, are you Jordan?'

He said it with no more effort than if he were talking to his neighbour, but his voice carried across the room.

'Yeah, that's right,' I said, with a sudden, jolting sense of regaining my identity.

'I have heard about you from Ruth. She is always saying you and I should get it together. Wow, your top is beautiful!' He put a hand on the fabric and then pointed towards his chest. 'Levan. Lev.' He enunciated all three syllables in the way his teacher might introduce a difficult word. Later that evening I found out that he was Georgian. Levan Tsereteli. An operatic name, to my ears.

'Levan is the Sunday name,' he said. 'Lev for every other day.' When I told him that he was the first Georgian I'd met he swelled a little, the great brows lifting.

'Oh, but you haven't got a drink.' He swept a hand across the table. 'What can I get you?'

'Oh, I'll stick to council juice.'

He frowned momentarily, his face dissolving into laughter when I explained I meant water.

He grabbed up a bottle, and as we chinked, he laughed again. 'Council juice!'

Language teachers are practised in the art of nodding and affirming in all the right places while at the same time internally running through our to-do lists. Our job is to shift the balance during the course of a lesson from Teacher Talking Time (TTT) to Student Talking Time (STT).

Meeting Lev that night, I forgot my training. There was something about him that made me open up. I found myself telling him things I'd told myself were trivial.

I told him of my week-long imprisonment in the classroom; I complained about the numbers of students and the fact that the roll appeared to grow every week. I told him about my colleague Simon with his seemingly permanent residency at the photocopier, of my tiny flat with its broken-down boiler that made it sound like there was someone trapped inside the pipes. Of the disgruntled taxi driver that evening (what I should have said: 'Excuse me, but is there a limit to the amount of information you're allowed to give me?')

I could hear my voice rising, and I had to check myself. I have never been that person: the one everyone avoids at parties. But I stuck to Lev that night. I needed to get everything up and out, and it was just his luck that his sensitive face was there for the moment of eruption.

The truth is: by the time I met Lev I had almost forgotten how people talk to each other socially. Maybe if I'd made a success of my life in London, I wouldn't have misjudged my relationship with him, built it up into something it wasn't.

I move the holdall through to Niall's bedroom, meaning to store it in one of his cupboards. Through the wall the hoover starts up. It breathes and gags as Niall pushes the nozzle into the furthest corners of the room. I wonder if he'll take a break from cleaning and fixing this evening. Maybe if I ask nicely he'll cook something, and we can sit in companionable silence in front of the box, maybe find a film. Like old times.

A couple of photographs on the sill: one a long, wide shot of Claire with Rebecca, taken a few years ago. She's young and open-faced, both arms wrapped around her child. Rebecca's plump cheeks touch her eyes. No longer a baby but not yet her own person.

When I visited five years ago, I arrived late from the airport to find Claire waiting but no Niall.

'Look, I've no idea when your brother's getting back. Shall we eat?'

We sat across from each other and Claire talked. She and Niall hardly went out these days, and she had taken to searching for her college friends on Facebook and listening to the music of her twenties on Spotify. She had devoted a Saturday morning to watching *Titanic*, while Rebecca was at a play date.

Eventually we heard the front door rattle, and a moment later Niall was there in front of us, his eyes searching and adjusting.

'Jordan?' His features made a dash for the centre of his face. 'You're winding me up. Claire! Did we say tonight?'

'I phoned a couple of times,' she said. 'I left messages.'

'Fuck, sorry mate.' Niall swayed into the room. 'No idea what I've done with my mobile.'

Claire's eyes never left Niall. As she was lowering the lid back down onto the tagine, he went very slowly to the sink, poured himself a tumbler of water and knocked it back.

He fell into a chair and the smell of whatever he'd been drinking joined us at the table.

'The wee bro. What do you think, Claire?'

She was by now standing in the doorway. She was looking at Niall as though he reminded her of someone that she couldn't quite place. She looked weary. Actually, she looked bored. She was bored of him, eager to get going, as though the only thing keeping her in that doorway and in that relationship was a huge effort of will.

Niall spun his head in either direction, trying to catch her up in his glance. He slumped to the side, his elbow just missing the table. He laughed like this was classic slapstick, like he was Keaton at his very peak.

That's the thing about Drunk Niall. He can be sweet and pathetic at the same time. It can be strangely endearing.

At least in the localised kitchen light I didn't have to look closely. In a couple of days, I thought, I'd be gone and then I wouldn't have to look anymore.

'Jordan!'

Niall, his voice nearly hoarse. I replace the picture of Claire and Rebecca on the ledge and just as I'm turning out of the room my mobile hums, warming my pocket.

I take out my phone and thumb the screen.

Great to see you last night...

I swipe across, tap in my passcode.

Great to see you last night after all these years. Coincidence or what?

I read it over once, then go back and rerun every word.

Coincidence or what?

I stare at the screen, trying to work out what I'm meant to say in reply.

If I'm even meant to reply.

Does a sentence with a question mark at the end always need an answer?

'Jordan!'

I close the cover of my phone and make a lurch across the hallway. Niall's poised at the headboard of Rebecca's bed.

'Into that corner,' he says, signalling with his head. 'Mind, now.'

He grips the edge of the headboard, glaring off. I believe he'd tidy me out of the way if he could. Bundled into the cupboard with the hoover and the rest of the cleaning stuff.

Coincidence or what?

I won't bother replying.

We lift the bed on three.

Great to see you last night.

I mean, what would be the point?

Niall pushes forward so hard that I stumble and let go my end.

'Are you trying to maim me?'

'Well, if you would only pay attention, Jordan…'

A quick reply couldn't hurt, could it?

'Off in your head, as always…'

David.

His face, ever alert.

Those arms.

I'll reply with a question, so he'll have to reply.

'Jordan.'

The light leaps in my brother's eyes as we lift again. I wipe my face expressionless, but my neck feels warm, as though it's soaked in the surprise of David's text.

Niall downs tools around eight and we wander across to Ocean Terminal. He nods towards the closed-down shops and the twenty-four-hour gym: he works out there a couple of times a week, he tells me, bashfully flexing one arm. We eat noodles in Wagamama's then board the escalator to the multiplex. The only film starting within the hour is *Red One*, which turns out to be a big special-effects number with The Rock and half a feature's worth of plot. We're restless, our hands colliding above the bag of Revels between our seats. Niall disappears and when he returns I can taste the second-hand smoke. He stretches out and yawns. We stifle our giggles with our fists. I start to wonder what we must look like to the folk around us, a pair of six-footers sliding around in our seats like the big bairns we are. It's a feeling I only just remember from childhood, this shared inanity.

When we were young we loved television – it was the one thing that united us as a family – and the best, the most *transcendent* times were when we gathered to watch a film. Sunday Westerns, weepies, comedies. These were the childhood souvenirs I've never grown out of.

I remember watching *The Wizard of Oz* for the first time, one Christmas, my mother wondering aloud how Niall and I could have reached the age we were without ever seeing it.

What do people picture first when they think of that film? The Munchkins, the Wicked Witch of the West, the ruby slippers? For me it was the cyclone that left the biggest impression, the idea that you could be lifted by a storm high into the air and dropped somewhere miles away and in glorious technicolour.

Watching Dorothy's house spinning towards Oz, I felt giddily along for the ride with her and Toto and Miss Gulch and the chicken coop. I would be okay, I told myself. It wasn't forever. I would put miles between myself and all of this. The bottles, these people, my family.

I just had to wait.

Davie

Poor boy's on the other side of the door, shrunk to a speck, stuck inside the peephole. I pull it open before I can change my mind.

And of course, straight away I get the dry mouth.

'Made it, then,' is all I can say.

'I must say, I didn't think we'd be seeing each other again quite so soon!'

He looks like he's hobbling a bit from the stairs. His shirt's made of crinkly stuff – expensive, I'm thinking. We smile at each other and start shifting around on the spot. I kind of want to hug him, and I'm not talking about a polite hug.

I try once again to interest him in a glass. It's good stuff this, from Cahors, France, liberated from Frank's rack, none of your pish. When he says no ('Bit early for me') I bust into the chocolates he's brought, holding out the box. There's fusty sweetness on his breath when he reaches for me.

Straight away he's pulling the front tail of my shirt, all kinds of excitement in his eyes. I take a step back and feel the sharp edge of the worktop. Jordan gives a tug and leads us out the room, making a beeline for the boudoir.

'Haud on,' I laugh, the vino jumping in my glass.

Part of me wants to take it easy. I spent the half hour before he arrived ironing this shirt. I changed the whole shape of my living room by lighting it only with lamps. I'd had notions of us sitting and talking in our good clothes in the nice light for a while. Pacing ourselves. Best laid plans.

By the time we get to the bedroom I'm just about drooling at the thought of my hand under the waistband of his pants, the bob of his cock. I could burst.

Easier this time, like taking a return trip, noticing sights along the way: the millions of grey hairs on his chest, that mole in the middle of his back that's a dead ringer for Iceland. We break off from time to time to laugh – at his creaking knee, me with my clicky shoulder. His neck goes red with every quick movement, and course I feel I've got to be all kid gloves.

The change in him when he comes is something else. It's like the life goes out of his eyes.

'I told my brother that we had... I mean, that I bumped into you again,' he says.

'I'm guessing he couldn't remember us either.'

'I remember you. I mean: I've been trying to *picture* you.' His mouth quirks. 'Sorry.'

Bat my hand to show him he's forgiven.

'I left school Christmas of... fifth year, I think it was,' I say. 'Meant to go back after the holidays and take some of my exams, but... you could say school and me weren't exactly made for each other.'

'I stayed right to the bitter end. Year two thousand—'

'Dinnae. Makes me feel old.'

'Same year we lost my dad.' He blurts the words. 'Sorry, I don't know why I said that out loud!'

He grins, but only just. And as I'm getting my mouth ready to say something, offer my condolences or whatever, he starts shaking his head.

'No. No, I mean, he'd been ill a long time.'

'A shite year for both of us, then?'

'You'll come back to me,' he says.

I don't want to come back to him. Even the thought of it makes my guts churn.

Still, I keep pushing, reminding him of it all.

'You mind Mr Mullan?'

'Oh, he was my English teacher. I think. Yes, Mullan, that was his name.'

'About the only class I could be bothered with in the end. Manky Mullan. Still see him around the place. He always looks at me funny like he's not sure if he should say hello.'

'I just remember him hiding in the book cupboard, crying.'

'Wife left him. Halfway through fourth year. He gave me a prize for a short story.'

All of a sudden I'm grinning. My greatest achievement. First prize in the annual story competition. The old boy came to the prize-giving suited and booted.

'What was the story about?' says Jordan.

'Oh... well, about a drug addict, and how they'd ODed in a bathroom at this massive party in a pop star's mansion in London, but you didn't know until the end that they were actually dead, and it was the corpse telling the story all along.'

'Very *Sunset Boulevard*.'

'How do you mean?'

'It's the same... device. The whole thing's narrated by a dead body floating in a swimming pool. You've never seen *Sunset Boulevard*?'

'I mean, I've *heard* of it.'

'Mr Mullan,' Jordan says. 'There's a blast from the past. You still write?'

'I mean, I've got a notebook. Used to scribble when the caff was quiet. I took creative writing classes a few years back, but... just... time, you know.'

I'd wanted to do something that would show Frank I was trying. You can do better, he kept saying. You're going to be a barista forever? You should be at the college.

Hence the classes, the notebook. I've just not got the staying power.

Jordan turns to his side, pulling the covers along with him, and I use the moment to budge closer.

'So, you're a teacher?'

'For my sins.'

'I could never do that. I'd be the one in the cupboard, greetin.'

'I've spent most of my career moving from place to place teaching adults how to speak English. It's not so terrible.'

'Sounds a decent life.'

'It has its moments.'

He grins and places a kiss on the side of my neck, and...

Fuck, that's nice.

'Do you remember that cartoon stuck on the wall outside the careers service at school?' He speaks slowly, almost to himself. '*You should learn how to play the guitar; it'll give you something to fall back on.* Remember? I didn't think much of it at the time, but now it sums up how I feel about teaching. I've spent twenty years teaching my backside off, refereeing arguments, trying to win trust, trying to maintain the whole tough-but-approachable persona that no teacher can carry off, not really, trying not to be exposed for the frightened... *child* I am.'

I watch his mouth. He's a talker, like Frank: he keeps on and on for fear some ghoulie comes in with the silence and scares the living shite out of him.

'Think I'll sign up to be a teacher.'

'Well, David, the profession always needs new blood—'

'Fuck that. Sorry... *cursing.*'

'I've heard swearing before.' He smiles, showing all those funny teeth. 'In multiple languages.'

'You been in France?'

'Marseilles. You been?'

'Told you, I never go anywhere.'

'Yes, and Spain, Prague.'

'And now?'

'London. Stoke Newington.'

'You're creeping back.'

'At this rate I'll be back just in time to take up my free place in the care home.'

'All that gallivanting…'

'I love it,' he says, his voice flat.

The chocs have found their way onto his knees. He eats the way he talks, without taking a breath, offering up the box just the once.

When he speaks again his tone's changed, shifted up a gear.

'Yeah, so I'll be heading off again on Monday.'

'Back to London?'

'The Big Smoke.'

'So this is a flying visit?'

'I suppose it is.'

He's quiet all of a sudden and I just lie there, trying to feel some kind of a way back in but actually saying fuck all. Can't tell him that I know fine well where Stoke Newington is, that I stayed there in a Marriott with Frank about a hundred years ago; we got pished on two-for-ones with a bunch of Dutchers in the bar on the second night. I was a ball of rage the next day. Hungover, desperate to get home – we'd had a long weekend of traipsing around.

I can't tell him that story because I haven't told him anything about Frank. So far I've kept that whole big part of myself to myself.

But Jordan's there beside me, and he looks okay, just lying there with his soft face still, quiet for once.

Worries me when he's quiet.

Scares me in a way.

So I make the whole thing a laugh. Bury my face in his neck, grab him around the waist. He pulls me in, holds me quite gently – you'd think we were married.

'Tell me something about Spain,' I say, and he starts up again, slow at first like he's reliving it all for the first time. Nicest people in the world, he says. Kindest folk you'll ever meet. He skips over details, wincing a bit as he goes back over the yelling fights he had with a Spanish boyfriend, and that leads him into telling me about the relationship he had with another teacher in France, which sounds like somebody's idea of perfect. Dinner, cinema, sex. They almost never saw each other in daylight.

'Dude was a vampire,' I say.

'Maybe.'

'Aye, maybe.'

'But listen to me,' he says, 'I'm the one doing all the talking.'

'My life's not all that, to be honest.'

What would be the point in telling him about Frank? Things might get heavy. He might get bored, get his legs going. I really don't want him to go.

He's looking hard at me. 'I can't believe you're half Spanish and you've never been to *Spain*.'

'Told you, I'm not the travelling type.'

'Never curious?'

'Nah,' I say, and then wonder if I mean it.

'Well, if you ever decided to go to Spain on one of those voyages of discovery, let me know and I'll hook you up with some friends.'

He puts his head on my arm, huffs out a sigh. I'm expecting him to look back up, keep going with his interrogations, and already my mind's working to find something interesting to say, or a memory that's real.

But then I hear his breathing get heavy. *Don't move*, I'm thinking, even though my arm's starting to go numb.

I settle back, quietly so as not to disturb, but my mind's busy.

This is the first time I've had someone fall asleep next to me since Frank.

There's a thought.

Sure, there've been meets through the summer: one-night wonders with no more meaning than wham-bam and not even a thank you man, none of which I've been able to make into stories, not yet.

Jordan Grieve, though.

Tonight, I've left the phone charging through the house. Like, right on the other side of the flat, with the sound off. If Frank wants us tonight, he can go fuck himself.

There's fighting talk. My heart pounding, taking the air out of me.

If I could only sleep like Jordan. Heavy like a wee bear.

Like Frank. Frank was a sleeper.

Some nights I dream Frank's name flashing up on the screen of my phone. It pulses in my head: *Frank, Frank, Frank*. Bullies me awake.

I roll onto my side, quiet as I can.

There were three in the bed and the little one said...

There was this thing I did. In a church basement at Holy Corner. Counselling. No kidding. Frank's idea. I'd been holed up in the spare room near enough two months, and I'd turned night into day. I prowled the house while he slept comatose on the other side of the bedroom door.

So, this counsellor started off telling me the time was mine. She wasn't there to give advice and I could say as much or as little as I wanted about what was on my mind at any moment.

And then she sits back.

Fucksake.

I felt the same panic I felt whenever I went to the surgery and the doc asked what was wrong. The old boy had drilled into me from the get-go that the GP's time was precious, and I should always try to be quick. Whenever my dad got sick, he'd get so tense he'd wait until he was in burning pain before darkening the surgery doors, convinced the doc would send him home with an instruction to get more fresh air and exercise.

My desire to not cry in that basement room was making me tremble inside.

'Well,' I said to the woman. 'I lost...'

'You *lost*...?'

'My other half... We split, you know.'

'I'm sorry to hear that. Had you and...'

'He.'

'Had you and he been together long?'

'Seventeen years.'

'Wow!'

'He was, *is*, a bit older than me.' I ploughed on. 'But, ah, that's not why I'm here. I mean, that's not the only reason.'

'Why *are* you here, David?'

'I'm here to talk about how I... feel.'

There was a question mark there at the end, just dangling, and the woman grabbed at it.

'You don't sound too sure, David.'

'I mean... I thought I was doing okay.'

'Do you talk to your family, David – your parents?'

'Mum died when I was four years of age. My old... my dad and I... We're no exactly what you would call...'

I brought up a hand to push my parents back out of the room.

'That's not – I'm not here for that.'

'Your friends? Why don't you tell me about your friends.'

I pictured Carol's tired face as she drove me across town that afternoon. We'd gone for a bite to eat the night before, me and Carol and all the troops. I was drinking. To be honest, I was pished. Part of me was there in the room with those folk, my pals.

Rest of me had checked out. I tipped the vino back, not to mention the vodka, turning the volume down on my wee queer family.

There was Dan and Luca, sitting so close they were just about in each other's laps. Carol, chewing her thumb to keep awake – she'd been up since six with the twins. Lazy bastard Cam flopped in his seat like he was in a deckchair, talking about this boy he'd met on hols. Evie with one leg over the arm of her chair, demanding of the room when we thought the next referendum might be. If Frank had been there something might have sparked. He loved chewing over the news. But the rest of us would only give shrugs and stares.

Carol kept asking was I okay.

Dan kept asking was I okay.

Luca kept asking was I okay.

Yes, I was okay.

'*I'm okay!*'

Maybe I used a curse word. Who knows. I've a sense the night ended badly.

The counsellor leaned her head.

'Suppose I don't want anyone worrying about me,' I said.

Well, she *loved* that.

'You're saying you don't want to upset your friends,' she said. 'And I can understand that. I hear that. But what about David? What about how David feels? What about David's feelings?'

I looked down towards my knees, so she wouldn't see me trying not to laugh. The floor was all pale wood, which made the place seem bigger than it was.

There was a low-down table with a box of tissues and a jug of water and glasses. Free-standing lamp in the corner. The chair I was sitting in was nice and comfy. And as I sat in that comfy chair in that white room, I wondered, if I asked nicely, if she might let me close my eyes and have forty winks.

I lifted my head again.

The counsellor was about my age. Her skin was shiny, the red on her cheeks flaring and calming like a warning light when she spoke. I felt sad as hell, having to sit in that silence. I wanted to make her day by saying something meaningful.

How do you feel, David?

How the hell did I feel?

A couple of thoughts came to me. They flashed up in my head like photos.

The first was Frank and I, naked as the day, clinging to each other on a single bed in a hotel room in St Petersburg: 2014, a decade ago, Christ. I was *sick* with relief when we got home. We'd managed to avoid even standing too close together, spooked by warnings about homophobia in the *Lonely Planet*. No kidding, I was a wreck. The hotel was cheap. Walls like sponge. We lugged in on the phone being answered in the reception, two doors down. We were paranoid the big bouncer in the lobby could hear us whispering sweet nothings to each other.

Next thought: Frank, knackered, eyes caked, saying he was going to cook. I started telling him not to bother. I'd make something, which meant an omelette, one of the three dishes I could manage without a flakey. But he looked sort of put out and so I went and opened a bottle instead.

We ate salmon with capers on the black bread he liked. For the main he'd brought out two lumps of venison. I pulled off my shoes. Listened to the knock of the knife. But the food wasn't coming, and it wasn't coming, and when I went through Frank was at the kitchen table with this funny look on his face. Funny meaning weird. Took me a minute to cop that he hadn't turned on the gas. I gently broke the news and he looked for a moment like he wanted to lamp me, which I didn't think was fair, and then that was him, he just slumped, and I felt his hurt down the wires of my own body.

But he kept going. That was Frank. The food, when we finally sat down to eat, was lovely, but he couldn't face it. He made a neat pile in the middle of his plate before raising himself and walking out the room.

I gave him a while then went upstairs, expecting to find him passed out. But he was standing at the window, eyes on the horizon, hands on the glass, and I asked him what I could do, but he wouldnae say anything, just shook his head.

How do you feel, David?

I feel...

I thought I'd move on. Shake him off. Feel free in a way. But there were days when it felt like he was everywhere around me. I took myself out for my long walks, aware of him in the corner of my eye. Stamped my feet to get the blood going, know. Tried to shock my body back to reality.

'I feel like I have to get going,' I said. 'The future.'

'Okay.' The counsellor nodding. 'Okay, good.'

Sometimes it was only a feeling, like a scribble on a page, and I could just about laugh and give myself a telling off. We made this decision together, Frank and me. We were uncoupling or decoupling or whatever it was, together.

But there were moments when the notion was bright in my head, that he was just sitting up there, rattling around the flat and needing me. And the idea got bigger, and the next thing I'd be back on the Willowbrae, back on the shining street. Standing on the other side from the flat, watching him go back and forth through the window.

'David?'

I was too hot, not just my face, all of me.

'I have to move on,' I said, my voice some kind of croaky.

The woman nodded with her eyes closed like she knew exactly what I was on about.

My time was up. I was out of there like a shot. I'd said all the stuff I thought she wanted to hear, and I would not be going back.

Beside me, Jordan lifts and drops.

Don't move.

I get up for a piss, quite nimble, then when I've done my business I creep the ten-odd steps to the living room. Pull free my headphones and scramble my fingers through the pile of CDs. *The Very Best of Kim Wilde*. There's a swing to the left, as the old boy used to say. Dust across the cover. Course I got Kim in the split. Frank hated any kind of cheesy pop.

On it goes. 'Kids in America'. Those juicy synths. I used to go nuts to this, back in the day. Now I can just about manage a few bars without my heart exploding, and just as Kim gets to the first chorus, I birl round and there's Jordan's giant face in the doorway.

'Jesus, what a fright.'

'Please don't stop on my account.'

Pull off my headphones. He's half dressed. Should have tied him to the bed.

'I need to get back,' he says.

'No sweat.'

He finds his shirt buttons.

'Um, listen, is it rude to ask…?'

'Aye. Probably.'

'Your soap bag in the bathroom…' He leaves a gap, choosing his words.

'Uh-huh?'

'You left someone. Or someone left you? I know, none of my business.'

'You're a real sleuth, you know? Regular fucking… Rebus.'

'How long…?'

'Few months.'

'Want to talk about it?'

'No really.'

'Well. I'm sorry.'

I look downwards at my wee dick hanging down. Cross my arms tight around my chest.

'Sorry,' he says again. 'Thing about me is, well, I never know when to shut up.'

'I like your shirt,' I say after a moment. 'I could never wear that.'

'Thanks.'

'Back to London, then?'

'My brother's couch first. London after that.'

'You're on the couch?'

'I know, look at the size of me!'

'He doesn't mind you sneaking off to meet me? Big bro?'

'He's... renovating. I get under his feet. Hence why I can't, you know, *host*. He thinks it's a good idea for me to get out and see my friends.'

'We hardly know each other.'

'I know.' He smiles.

He could stay a wee bit longer and take me out of myself. Maybe if I said please he'd hold my head in his hands until I fall entirely asleep.

'So, when are you...?'

'Monday. Early doors.'

He moves towards me, and I lean into him. Tomorrow's fuzz is just beginning to make a faint line around his mouth. I want him to stay. I even mouth the word, but if he stays he might recognise the boy with the hat pulled down over his ears who used to stand around on the edges, watching Hutton and the rest kick shit out of him. Hating and loving that whole show. Never once piping up.

'Better go,' he says into my neck. 'I'm due at my mum's tomorrow.'

'See you in another twenty-odd years?'

I follow him through the flat. He turns suddenly on the landing and leans back through the doorway, aiming a kiss. I'm not expecting it and so we bring our heads together, *boof*.

'We're bad at this, aren't we?'

'Terrible. Bye-bye, David.'

Sorry.

I whisper it as he disappears downwards.

I'm sorry.

He used to walk around with his chin up, this Jordan. Dignified, you'd call it, even when the back of his coat was running with snot. Never a bleat usually, but this one time – Hutton had spent the whole of biology pinging his ears – he got up from his seat calm as you like and sent Hutton with a full-on belt to the pus. Not a jab or a punch, a real soap opera of a slap. Knocked the bastard for six.

What I felt, the... *elation*, I can't tell you.

What was the problem, Petri Dish wanted to know.

Some clype raised a hand. 'I believe Hutton Kern called Jordan a...'

'A what?'

'Gay. He called Jordan a... gay.'

'Oh, for god's sake.'

Jordan just sat there, his face closed.

Petrie's cheek twitched.

'It's a word you hear a lot these days,' she said. 'When I first started in this job that word meant something quite different.' The smile broke wide. 'Yes, I am that old.'

The whole class laughed. I didn't trust myself to look at Jordan.

I sit for a while after he's gone. I could sit here scuddy until the cobwebs start gathering. Is this not the life, after all? The freedom to do fuck all?

If I didn't check in, would Frank or Carol come round, bust the door, howl over my remains?

I push the switch. My headphones have come loose, so Kim comes back on, shouting the odds, and because it's stupid o'clock and even her from next door's telly's off I click the button and the rest is hospital silence.

The lamps make the room cosy. Maybe this place isn't such a shithole after all. I'll paint the flat, get my stuff back from Frank and settle in here. Might even put up some Christmas decs. Fake tree, the works.

Decision.

I'll have changed my mind another twice before morning.

Near enough one-thirty. I keep looking across at my phone where it's plugged in on the other side of the room, the wee light glaring back. God knows how many times I do the same thing, over and over and over.

Enough.

And then, right on cue: *ding.*

No fucking way. I sort of brush my hair to the side with my hand, look around for my undies, like the doorbell's gone and I've been caught on the hop.

Uncoupling.

We're meant to be uncoupling.

I cross the floor but stop short of picking up my mobile. Floor creaking either side as I rock on my tippy toes. I've got a hand cupped around my knackers like he can see me. In my mind he's sitting with his phone in his hands waiting impatiently.

Not tonight, Frank. I hustle for the door just as the dinger goes again. Tetchy wee reminder. For all my determination I stay frozen in the doorway.

I could be in bed for all he knows. Or it might just be Carol, wanting the latest. I feel a dick, up and down like this, but I can't help looking, wanting to hear the dinger go again but not willing to make the next move, and nothing new from him either.

I lean against the door, trading looks with my phone.

'Not tonight,' I say, out loud, but I don't move.

Jordan

This past decade my mother has lived in her mother's house. When my grandparents moved in at the end of the seventies the brand-new bungalow touched the southern city boundary. Nothing but woods beyond. It might as well have been the end of the earth. Now it sits somewhere inside a maze of estates that sprawls all the way to the bypass.

This house has always been a refuge. We came for sleepovers and my grandad swaddled us in blankets that gave off sparks whenever we moved. Since my gran's death, Mum has cloistered herself in three rooms. When I spend the night, I sleep in the cubby through the back. A dog-eared Agatha Christie sits permanently on the chest of drawers by the bed. *Sleeping Murder.* I'll flick through it tonight, for comfort's sake, before turning out the light. Its first few pages have a soporific effect, right enough.

I sit on a stool while she works at the cooker. Through the window the sky is being pulled at its edges into ribbons of blue and white. I'd like to stay here for the next hour, watching the slow fade to black. I've sat on this stool by this window so often and at so many heights, only now I don't have to stretch my toes to reach the floor. I have the usual view of the garden: my grandad's gift to the world. Mum keeps it alive, crowded with colour.

Her back's fine, she assures me. She can't complain. She's thinking of repainting the front room and putting down a new carpet. The television's rubbish but she has plenty of books. She goes to the nursing fellowship on a Thursday, and she's been at the retirement complex twice this week. She still takes Jean Bremner for a run in the car every other Friday because her daughter lives in the Algarve now. Jean's near ninety; she's amazing for her age.

'You're looking well, Mum.'

'I'm what?'

She wears dark trousers and a cream cardigan. She might be all dressed up for an evening at the complex if it weren't for the striped butcher's apron. A ragged thing: Niall made it in Home Economics in his first year at the big school.

She's made fish pie, which she still thinks of as a favourite. I feel my conscience twitch as I dig out my first prawn, trailing a length of cheese. I could never eat any kind of meat or fish in front of Lev. Even the thought of eating dead animal repulsed him. Okay, so maybe it's not the end of the planet if I occasionally swallow a prawn or a square of cod, but Lev wouldn't see it that way.

Mum sits at the other end of the table and lifts her fork. She chews every mouthful at least a dozen times. *Your stomach doesn't have teeth*: her mantra to us when we were kids. She said we never let the food touch the sides of our bellies.

She inhales now, readying herself to ask after my brother. I know the signs of old. Lowered eyes, a heaving breath. As a teen, I would be taken aside and asked for a report, even if he'd only just left the room. She was always preoccupied with Niall. Our conversations were more like reports filed at the end of a long day of surveillance.

'He seems well enough. He's still off the... Six months he's been off the...'

Mum blinks down at her plate, and there's another deep breath. I keep going, skipping to the next thought: 'You know, he's made a nice job of Rebecca's room.'

'Good for him,' she says. 'He's had his battles, but he's... a good sort at the end of the day. He loves that girl.'

I had wakened early this morning, but Niall was already up and ready to go in his painting clothes, sitting at the kitchen table with his laptop open. I watched his lips move as he took in the crossword clues, breaking off now and then to hammer out his answers.

'Right, genius, what's this one: seven down, seven letters: "Deems proper".'

I peered over his shoulder. Next to the puzzle site was another open browser tab: *Select Dating: Your Love Life Begins at Forty*.

'Seven letters... "Fitting"?' I said, turning away from the screen.

'That means fourteen across is wrong.' He pulled the lid down, pushed his laptop aside. 'Crosswords are for... *gimps*.'

He turned his energies to making poached eggs with spinach, and we ate together with Forth burring away in the background. There was a movie quiz, and we both shouted the answer at the same time. *Only Angels Have Wings!*

'What time's Claire dropping off Rebecca tomorrow?' I asked.

'Ah, well now, Claire phoned,' he said. 'Change of plan.' He saw my frown. 'No no, now, everything's hunky dory, she's just a bit under the weather. A bug. Something that's going round. Claire's going to drop her off Sunday instead. It's okay, she's okay. Gives me a bit extra time to finish off her room. You know, get it just right. And then she'll be here!'

He pushed his chair back, whisking up our plates, not so brittle and clenched as he'd been the day before.

On the way out the door I stuck my head into Rebecca's bedroom. Niall was already hard at work. The latest additions were a green-fringed rug to go with the feature wall, soft toys of indeterminate species arranged in a group hug at the end of the bed and a shelving unit full of books. Cushions, cushions everywhere. If Niall made any more improvements there would be no room for the child herself.

'Haven't seen Rebecca for months,' my mother says now. 'They used to leave her with me every Saturday morning.' A smile comes into her eyes. 'Well, she's at that age. Always on the go. Wee friends. You know. You're lucky if she has time to come to the phone. You and your brother were the same at that age.'

She means Niall, not me. The idea that I was once that kid with the full dance card is hilarious.

She lowers her head, returning to her food.

'Hey, Mum, you know what I thought about on the train up? Remember when Rebecca was born? The day she was born. Remember? She arrived first thing. You were still living in the flat, and I came to stay. Neither of us could sleep. You got up at five and started cleaning the kitchen. We had breakfast together at half six. And then Niall phoned...'

She pauses in her chewing. Despite the odd line and the heavy glasses she's taken to wearing, she's retained a certain innocence about the eyes. Or maybe it's puzzlement. She always did look bewildered when confronted with a question from her other son.

'Course I remember.'

My mother prides herself on being sharp. She complains at length about the old folk at the complex who can barely remember their own names – as though they're deliberately playing up to some unhelpful stereotype of the elderly.

'Yes, so, I'll need to be going down to the infirmary later on this week,' she says.

'Oh?'

'Mr Wojtowicz's not too well. Trouble with his insides.' She stabs the crust of her pie. 'I've been taking Mrs Wojtowicz down to see him. She's not driving now.'

'They must be some age.'

'He's eighty-six and she's eighty-seven. They're going to give him a colonoscopy, see if they can get to the bottom of it.'

As it were.

'You're good to them, Mum.'

'It's nothing they wouldn't do for me, if they were able.'

She focuses on her plate, lifting each of the many little forkfuls to her mouth with something like the same care and attention she pays to the Wojtowiczs and Jean Bremner and all the other people she has taken under her wing in her time.

When my mother taught piano – which she did for years – the house at Drumbrae was a bustling place. She had trained as a nurse, taking time out when she had Niall, and then me; she started teaching as a way of bringing in extra cash. She soon had to turn people away because her lessons were cheap. She never did more in the way of advertising than sticking up a notice in the nearby branch of the Co-op.

Her pupils came in a steady stream, which meant Niall and I were usually kept away from the living room after school. We let ourselves in the back door, commandeering the kitchen in the name of homework, raiding the cupboards, bickering with our mouths full.

Sometimes I would sit on the stairs and read while listening to the thumped scales, the stumbling efforts at Bach. The piano was an old upright the landlord had left behind along with some bashed furniture when his own mother decamped to a home. The word *DEUTSCHLAND* stood out in faded gold above the keyboard. I remember the introductory pieces she would assign to differentiate between the major and minor keys, 'Merrily We Roll Along', which was as cheerful as its title, and 'The Sandman', which was the stuff of nightmares.

Whenever one of the kids began to run out of steam, my mother would take to the keys and play something jaunty. 'There's a hole in the bottom of the sea,' she sang. 'There's a hole, there's a hole, there's a hole in the bottom of the sea.' It was meant to be cheerful, something to rescue the lesson, but I found the very idea a scary one.

At night I lay awake while Niall breathed below. What hole? Where did it go? The image in my head was of a lacuna filled with blackness or a dizzying drop to nowhere.

I had always had problems getting to sleep. When I was tiny, I'd tried so hard to get out of my cot that I ended up battering my chin off the bars. My dad called it separation anxiety, which brings to mind a rescue dog. Some nights he would sit with me in his lap beside the electric fire until he was absolutely certain I wouldn't move or wake.

This all sounds fanciful now. That clinging child is gone. I have no idea who he was or when the real me arrived, like a changeling, to oust the original from the top bunk.

It was Dad who broke the news that our mother would be going back to work in the geriatric ward at the Royal three shifts a week. He stalked around the subject the way he had done when he gave the talk about wet dreams and pubic hair, rambling in circles, without looking me in the eye.

'It'll mean more money coming in,' he said. 'But your mother might get tired sometimes – she'll have a lot on her plate.'

In fact, the return to the wards rejuvenated her. We were used to seeing her in the sober blacks she wore when she gave lessons. Now the greens and blues of her uniform brought out the colours in her eyes. The piano sat unloved in its corner. I made a point of wiping down the dust once a week and sorting through the piles of papers and mail that collected across the lid and stool. Walking my fingers up and down the keys, wishing I could play.

*

'Listen. Bed's made up in the back,' she says as I clear the table. 'I wasn't sure how long you'd be wanting to stay. You're staying, are you?'

'That's the plan.'

'Okay.' She brushes an imaginary something off her cardigan, turning to look at the flowers I brought, still in their sleeve on the counter.

'These are lovely,' she says. 'I'll get them in water.'

Niall and I have tried without success over the years to repay, in some small way, the things our mother did for us when we were growing up. Gifts embarrass her. Treats are for other people. Christmas presents are acknowledged with a nod and a cursory examination – 'No, I do like it. I really am very fond of that colour...' – only for the sweater or scarf to disappear into the back of a cupboard, joining the pile for the next charity pick-up.

When Niall and Claire and I took her to a restaurant one birthday she sat in her seat for fifteen minutes before taking off her coat. The look of disquiet on her face when she asked the waiter what a focaccia was made me want to climb on my chair and announce to the room that I didn't know what a focaccia was either.

'Listen. I don't *need* anything, Jordan,' she has said. 'If you're out there living your life then I'm the happiest woman in the world.'

The one and only time I brought a boyfriend home for Christmas, some time ago now, she seemed to regress. Or perhaps she felt as though we were all too much for her, me and Niall and Claire and Juan Andres, like we were children again, rushing around her legs.

Juan Andres won her over, as I knew he would. He had the right instincts, a gentle manner with people. He had seen that my mother was intimidated by the occasion, and so he knew to soften his voice, take things at her pace.

Before she left she took me aside.

'You've found yourself a nice friend there, Jordan, and I'm so happy for you. Now you hang on to him.'

And I was so pleased. I felt almost intoxicated with happiness.

Two years later, when Juan Andres and I had broken up and I was making plans to move to France, I broke the news to my mother on the phone.

'Well, that's a shame,' she said, in a tone I remembered from childhood, when one of us had been careless and broken some precious toy, or if she had heard us using *language*.

'Oh no, it's fine. Really. I'll be okay.'

'Well, I can't help feeling it's a real pity. He was good for you.' She paused, in search of the right words. 'He looked at you like he was interested in everything you had to say.'

At nine, when she gets up to turn on her programme, I go through to the room my gran used to call the Very Front, the one kept for good. Some things have stayed constant, like the press cut into the wall, but the room seems small and very bare. There is no piano. All my grandparents' treasures – the figurines and the carriage clock, the vases of different shapes, the kissing Dutch boy and girl – are long gone to charity. I used to love this kitsch stuff with all my heart, but my mother was never sentimental about bits and bobs.

I trail my fingers along the few paperbacks, then lower myself onto the carpet and pull out one of the cardboard storage boxes from the bottom shelf. The lid comes free on the second tug. At the top is a stack of Rebecca's school photos. Flicking through them, I watch her age, from four to nine. Her expression is at its most inscrutable in this latest picture. What's going through her head? Embarrassment? Contempt? She has eyes that seem almost too much for her head to contain. Like Niall. Like our father. Like me.

The folder at the bottom contains my school photos. The year's carved into the topmost cardboard frame: 1999. There I am, in the back row in the middle, the second tallest boy in my class, my face revealed through curtains of hair.

I'm seventeen in the picture, smiling like a beauty queen. I spent a lot of time smiling at that age. My smile (on closer inspection a show of teeth with nothing in the eyes) was the sign I hung on my face to tell the world I was fine.

Mum and Niall would tease me for the amount of time I spent smiling, not really engaging.

'You've got cloth lugs,' Niall said when I didn't answer him. 'You've got the blinkers on.'

I spent hours on my homework, writing everything out multiple times to keep from having to engage with my family. The phrase *Earth to Jordan* wore diaphanous with use.

'Excuse my brother,' Niall would say to the friends he invited over. 'He's here in body, if you know what I mean.'

'He's all right,' said Mum. 'He just lives in his own wee world.'

I smiled wide and bright.

'He's fine,' my dad said. 'You're fine, Jordy.'

In a way, family life was something that went on around me. In dreams of my childhood, I'm watching them from behind glass.

It was around this age, sixteen, seventeen, that I started to run. It became as much a necessity as sleeping or eating. Weekends I could keep my pace up for hours, discovering places I didn't even know existed as the light changed around me. I felt almost weightless, carrying nothing, except maybe a key tied to my shoelace.

In photos from that time, you can see the difference it made in me, my shoulders narrowing, my face deflating.

It began as flight, from the boys who sat nearby, whose voices were always in my ear. I smiled to show I didn't care. There was something satisfying about the noise my teeth made when I held them together.

At bell time, I would rise and walk away, my bag secured to my back, my core tightening, fired up, so that when I reached the playground and the shouts and thundering hooves drew closer, I was ready to go, the Rocketeer. It was like taking to the skies.

They caught up with me a few times, pulling me by the jersey, tackling me to the ground. They didn't know what to do next, not really, so mostly they just left me there in the dirt, and walked away, grunting and shoving each other's shoulders.

Once, though, I stopped. I turned. I could see the confusion on their faces as they got nearer. There was something cold in me that day. I squared my body and barrelled forward. I plunged into the group.

They punched and kicked mainly below the waist but one of them caught me across the face with his watchstrap and my lip split so deep it ran red.

But it was the torn sleeve of my coat that held my mother's attention.

'I wish you would try to fit in at that school,' she said as she stitched the wounded garment.

Niall overheard our parents talking about what had happened. Dad wanted to go up and see the Head, but Mum was reluctant to make a fuss over what she said was a bit of rough and tumble among a group of lads.

Later on, I caught my father looking at me across the table. That night as we watched television he reached for me without a word and pulled my head onto his lap, whispering something I couldn't quite hear.

Now I watch Mum through the doorway as she makes tea for herself. She opens a drawer for biscuits. There are unopened packets in there, bought for my visit. Penguins, Breakaways, Clubs. Mum's not a sweet tooth but she knows I'm a girl who can't say no. Her air of good humour makes me wonder why I've stayed away so long. I wonder if she remembers that episode with the torn coat: if she really knew what was going on, and whether she considered it to be anything more than horseplay. As I watch her I can feel the memory – so vivid a moment ago – splinter and fall away, like a lost dream.

Now she's pouring me a glass of milk. Only in my mother's house could I get away with drinking cold full-fat milk. I'll go through and sit with her, watch the end of her series and drink milk and eat Penguin biscuits.

I have a memory of waiting for her one evening in town. I'd taken the bus after school, for Christmas shopping and to take pictures: indiscriminate close-ups of buildings, gates sparkling with frost, graffiti on walls, pigeons eating out of bins, spiderwebs stretched across railings. It was my hobby at the time – photography was the height of cool as far as I was concerned. But I was cold and had been relieved to take shelter inside Thin's, opening paperbacks and searching through opening lines.

I was always a fast reader, and there had been a lot of practice in the school library. I'd read my way through the single-shelf section marked Scottish Literature and belatedly realised how predictable our family was in many ways, how unsurprising its reticence and drinking men. My other hideout was the school darkroom, which was warm and quiet, a literal closet.

Mum was running late, and I was starting to wonder if I'd got the wrong meeting place. As I was turning to head outside, my stomach tightened, seemingly for no reason, and all of a sudden they were there, three or four or five or maybe twelve teenage boys in blue sweaters with the black and yellow crest, ties crudely knotted.

I tried to edge out of the frame, but it was too late. There was an odd moment of what seems now like choreography. 'Jordy-boy!' came the cry as they crowded round.

The heavy, lumbering boy. Let's call him Gavin. The second of them was tall, slim-faced with toffee-dark skin, his hair buzzed close to his head. Why not call him Gary. There were others, Wullie and Boab and Soapy Souter and Eck, who can remember.

'Nice camera, Jordy.'

The buzzcut reached for the strap of my camera bag. I took another step back, and he made another grab for the strap, yanking me towards him. I tried to back away, pulling him with me, and collided with the bookshelf.

'Jordan!'

My mother was suddenly there. She made her way past a group of primary school kids and their mums rummaging for stocking fillers. She was in her work uniform under the navy coat that she wore every winter for years. She frowned as the boys turned, a snake-quick spasm.

'I was waiting over by the door, Jordan,' she said.

There was something different about her voice, a rising-and-falling quality to the intonation. I'd never heard that voice from her, but I recognised the stick-on smile.

'Excuse us, please.' One of the mums squeezed past, forcing us to widen the circle. We were quite a posse now, this strange group bunching around the bookshelf. I found myself standing close to Gary with the buzzcut. He smelled like a gym bag.

'Jordan?'

People were sidestepping between us.

'Mrs... uh, we were just asking Jordan if he wanted to go for a pizza with us so we could talk about, you know, homework and things.'

That was Gavin, the ringleader.

My mother leaned away, holding the front of her coat closed. She half turned, opening up a small gap between herself and the group. But then, just as Gavin was starting forward, she angled her shoulder around again, reasserting the barrier and forcing him to take a step back into the cushioning arm of his pal.

'It might be better if you make it another day,' she said.

There was some muttering, a noise of bags being hitched onto shoulders, and the boys swung away between the displays.

My mother watched them bump through the door and out into the night. We pretended to look at the shelves, murmuring something about gift ideas, until we were sure they'd gone. She didn't say anything, and I didn't thank her.

I remember when I came out to her. Actually, I didn't have to do anything. News of my relationship with a boy I'd met in my first year at university wound its way up the east coast, eventually reaching our mother's ears. Someone who knew the boy let it slip to someone else who happened to know a girl I was at school with who told her mum who mentioned it to her colleague who happened to be Mum's friend (Auntie Liz) who gently but spitefully broke the news.

I was home for a rare weekend and Mum was making coffee. There was a variety of biscuits. She'd been asking the usual questions – how was my course going, what were our digs like, did I have enough money, was I making friends?

'What's this I hear about you going out with the boys?'

Her tone was devil-may-care. She tried to speak again but all she could do was shake her head. A moment later she had to sit down, and once composed she started on one of her dreamy monologues.

'Listen, there was this woman at work...'

She snapped an Abernethy, weighing up the two halves as though deciding whether she really wanted to tell the story.

'We weren't great friends really,' she said. 'We went for lunch together a few times and she used to walk me up the road after a shift. Wendy. She was a good pair of ears. Sometimes we'd sit in the bus shelter outside the hospital for ages, just blethering and watching the smokers. She was divorced and only saw her daughters at weekends.'

I stood with my coffee, not wishing to interrupt. I might have been holding my breath.

'When I told her about your dad – I mean, about how he kept getting *smaller* and, I don't know, smaller – this Wendy, she looked at the ground. Then she reached over and put her head against my head, and I thought for a moment I was going to *cry*.'

She shot a glance at me.

'But then she wanted me to go away on holiday with her and I said no. I mean, I thought about it. I mean, what harm, really...? But in the end I couldn't. I was embarrassed about what had happened, so I kept my distance from her. No more lunches, no more walks. And then she left for a new job in... Liverpool, I think it was, or Blackpool. We had a wee party in the nurses' station before she left. I went home and watched Peter, your dad, Pete, slowly sliding down in his chair and wondered if I'd done the right thing. One week, somewhere warm. Suddenly all I wanted was for someone to put their head against my head the way she had.'

She looked up.

'You're sure you're okay, Jordan?'

I realised only when she spoke to me directly that we were still in the same room.

'Of course, you'll be fine,' my mother said. 'You've always been your own person.'

That bleary enquiry in her eyes.

'Oh, Mum,' I managed, and I'm not even sure she heard.

No more was said, of course, though Niall relished telling me that Mum had spent the evening on the couch looking at old photos.

He wanted to know what had happened. I told him Mum was all over the place because she'd found out her son was a shirtlifter. Niall couldn't see what all the fuss was about. 'Now if you'd told her you were a shoplifter...'

'Jordan? You're all right through there, are you?'

An edge to her voice. She doesn't know why I'd want to go raking around. The past belongs in boxes, with the lid on, hidden away in a room she never uses.

Oh dear, here's a picture of my father, taken before I was born. He's standing in Holyrood Park. The light is poor, and the image is a little blurry, the flash on my mum's old point-and-shoot too weak to reach its target. An avenue of trees with half-naked branches on either side; a glimpse of the palace wall on the left. Orange and brown leaves pushing all the way to the bottom of the picture. His hands are loose at his side and his head's back, and he's laughing. Laughing, I imagine, at Mum trying to remember not to put her thumb over the lens.

I can't picture what he'd look like now. I won't come close to knowing, I suppose, until Niall or I are older, and the mirror shows us an approximation of what we want to see.

I knew from an early age my father drank. The smell was a given – it was a part of him. The house was often full of his acquaintances, sitting around the living room, inhaling the dregs out of cans and laughing their laughter that ended in coughing fits.

It wasn't until my teens that I realised he was a drinker more than he was an electrician or a father or even a man. He no longer danced around the kitchen with the broom or did any of the things that had once tickled us. Niall, who was on the cusp of adulthood, ceased watching the Hibs with him. Dad missed appointments, lost jobs.

Mornings, topping up his tea with Bell's, he would sit in jersey and shorts at the kitchen table or in the living room, turning the pages of a days-old newspaper. He kept bottles in every part of the house: behind books, down the side of the sofa, lodged in cushion covers.

He had turned into an obstacle the rest of us had to negotiate. Niall barked at him to move if he was searching for his boots or a book he needed for school. If Mum was studying or giving the house a clean, she would politely ask him to shift from one part of the house to another. This he did, with difficulty, creaking out of his chair.

My mother would often talk about Niall or me to her colleagues, but she didn't think to mention Dad. Sometimes she would invite home one or two of the student nurses for a scratch meal and they would stand in the corner, confusion tripping their faces while she squeezed around this man, her husband, like he was a piece of furniture.

The pair of them, Niall and Mum, began shuttling me in and out of rooms my father was entering or leaving. I wasn't daft – I knew he was on the slide. They would usher me off to bed early, but the sound of Niall giving Dad a hard time in the living room rose all the way to my top bunk.

Later, when he was gone, my mother seemed in a way to wake up. Like Dorothy but in reverse, returning home to a world of fun and colour. Her friends came and went. They went on trips to the theatre and cinema. Sometimes there would be a riot in the living room. One night I pushed the door and saw Mum and half a dozen others, sitting in a close circle. They were discussing a mutual friend who kept banging on about immigration and the foreign nurses who were taking all the jobs.

'One of these days, I'll come right out with it,' my mother was saying. '"Susie," I'll say, "You live in Stocky. It's not exactly swamped."'

Gales of laughter. I had never heard her hold court like that. I wanted to record my mother's voice, the vibrancy in it, play it to Niall.

'You hear that? Garbo laughs!'

I can feel her now, her slender presence, in the doorway behind me. I turn and we smile at each other across the gap.

'I was just coming to... I've got biscuits needing used up.'

In the kitchen, the flowers are on the counter, still wrapped tight. As she places the cup and plate in front of me the landline bleats, and she startles me with her animation.

'Niall,' she says, leaning for the receiver.

Ten o'clock on the dot. This is a nightly thing; I've seen Niall counting down to the hour, repeatedly checking the time.

I watch her get comfy in her chair.

I sit for a while, the third wheel, occasionally glancing over at my mother's attentive face. I stretch for a biscuit then take out my phone and spend a lot of time staring down at David's name. After yesterday, I told myself that was that, but he wouldn't leave off: his listening face, the generous kiss. This afternoon, as the bus rattled through the city, he was a perpetual presence, as real and vivid as the man sitting next to me.

It takes a while to decide what to type, everything possible in that moment of indecision.

Don't suppose you're free tomorrow evening?

Kiss.

No kiss.

I press send before I can change my mind, and suddenly I'm eighteen again, my heart in my throat. I affect a light tread as I putter past Mum to the back room.

'Off to bed,' I mouth to her.

'You not saying night-night to your brother?'

'Nighty-night.'

She giggles like a kid into the receiver.

I throw myself onto the mattress and take out my phone, look down at his name again and there's an instant reaction, a mix of hard-on and heart flutter. At the same time, I know there's something glossy about the image I hold in my head, as though I could open my eyes and realise with a start that David is something I've made up. The picture blurs, and Lev's face replaces David's. Lev, staring, frowning.

I think there has been a misunderstanding.

A week from now I'll be back in London and David will be moving on to his whatever comes next, putting his breakup behind him. We might bump into each other in another couple of decades, when our joints are rusting, and our memories have become vaguer than ever. Will I find him sexy then? Maybe we'll chat briefly then go on our way, wondering what it was we ever saw in each other.

I churn through *Sleeping Murder*, and when I give up, I drop the book onto the floor and turn my attention to the ceiling. A creak, and my mother is there in the room telling me that Niall wonders what time I'll be back tomorrow.

'He's so excited about having you over, it's lovely, really. You're good for each other,' she says, padding away, and at that moment my phone gives its little jolt.

What time were you thinking?

In the night the wind gets up, and it hurls itself at the window, and I pull the covers tighter and lie there, thrilled by the romance of it. Where will the wind carry me next?

Over the years I have tried to get to the Emerald City many times, setting out with the necessary amount of hope, eventually finding myself back at the start of the Yellow Brick Road, with my sights set on a new cityscape. Marseilles, Prague.

London now.

My original thought had been to move to Brighton. A colleague from Spain had landed there and had been sending delighted emails ever since. It was a vibrant place; it was by the sea. He already had a network of friends. But there was a job going at the college in Stoke Newington, with tied accommodation. As with every other move I'd made in the past twenty years, I took a leap. Brighton wasn't a million miles away from London. On the map of England everything looked close together.

On my first day at school, the head of department had paraded me through the staff room, clapping the other teachers to attention and announcing the arrival of fresh blood.

'Come and meet Mr Grieve, everyone!'

A few muted hellos. I stood around the beige-and-black room, smiling at the edges of conversations I hadn't been invited to join.

That set the pattern. This was not like the other schools I had worked in. Elsewhere, everyone was an outsider, so people gravitated towards each other. There was an easy, holiday atmosphere, people looked out for each other. Friends became family, albeit an ephemeral, oddly low-stakes type of family.

In London, I felt my age in a way I never had before. Here, the middle-aged teachers were coupled up. They had mortgages, kids, social lives outside of work. Any single colleagues I had were on dating apps and looking, hard. The only other gay man in the department was semi-retired and planning a move to one of the pretty shires.

Even in the parks where I went running there was a feeling of people, couples, dogs, all turning away from me. Souls, bodies everywhere, but I had never felt more alone.

For a while, I made the effort. I accepted invitations from some of the younger teachers to their pubs on Fridays and told them the soda water I'd sneaked from the bar was gin-and-tonic. In France, Spain, Prague, I could get away with sitting for hours nursing a cranberry juice. Here, as the most senior by far, I felt obliged to pay my share. My wallet bled. I hadn't been around this much desperate Friday night drinking since my teens.

The turnaround of students was high. The more committed ones opened up about their lives. On their breaks they took turns to collect coffee from the always-full pot in the kitchen and they bitched about the cost of living. Sometimes, without notice, they disappeared, scunnered by the problem of the English language. New faces came in to take their place. They all blurred together after a while. For a while at least, I would be the mainstay, the fixture with the fixed grin.

I craved connection. I started thinking about my mother, Niall, Rebecca. Not for the first time, I started wondering what it would be like to go back to Kansas.

But there was Lev. Lev, who sought me out a few days after Ruth's party, tapped me on the shoulder in the canteen.

'Maybe you would like to take a coffee?'

It was high time I made a friend, and so we began sitting together at lunchtimes. There were gaps in our understanding but somewhere between his imperfect English and my fluency in hand signalling we were able to work out what the other meant.

From the ages of twelve to twenty-five Lev had fantasised about getting out of Georgia. He longed to escape the large family living together in the long, narrow flat. The curious neighbours, the stifling community.

When I asked what the country was like he threw out a reply. Oh, it was beautiful, the old buildings, the lakes, the surrounding mountains. These were lines he had learned down pat for his English classes. His father had wanted him to go into business or science, but Lev loved music, dancing, learning languages. He had stood his ground and gone into the humanities faculty at the state university.

'Let me tell you the most important thing. I wanted to meet...' He glanced around. 'It was at the university that I first met... *queers*.'

The word made me flinch. But Lev rolled it around in his mouth like a boiled sweet. *Queers*. He gave a side-giggle, his eyebrows rising, and I saw then that he shared my need to talk.

Tbilisi was changing, he told me, but Georgia was a tough place to be gay. There were boys he liked, but he'd been too scared to make an approach. Friends had been disowned or exposed or worse for coming out. Some had left Georgia for Germany, Italy, Istanbul. Lev had been teased throughout his childhood. Others had been harassed, beaten up. One had been attacked, dragged into the boot of a car by a group of boys and driven around for what seemed like hours before being dumped by the side of a road, miles from home.

He looked at me and shrugged. He was smiling, his eyes were sad, and I didn't have words. When I excused myself and walked across the canteen to the toilets I realised my hands were shaking. In the cubicle, I threw up into the bowl, and then had to sit on the bathroom floor, silently reading the homophobic comments scrawled across the walls.

Lev had so many passions, it was exhausting to keep up. He had long dreamt of coming to England because he loved music: the Beatles, Stone Roses, Blur; a whole lot of other bands I'd never heard of. He was teaching himself to play guitar with a program he'd downloaded because he couldn't afford to pay for lessons. He loved singing. He was interested in environmental issues, organising litter picks at the weekends and pouring scorn on the students who brought their cars to campus.

Lev held his cup to his chin. He was grateful to his sister and brother-in-law for giving him the box room in their house in Zone 4, but he was eager for change, tired of being confined to his room while domestic life raged on the other side of the door.

'I am still like an adolescent, do you see? Always the teenager in his room, trying to hide from the family.'

He wanted to travel: France, Germany, Scandinavia. He was curious about Scotland and asked me why we didn't vote for what he called our freedom.

I barely answered, beyond smiling.

In the run-up to the referendum my friends in Prague kept asking me about the vote and I had only shrugged, ambivalent as ever about home, more bemused than anything. But then I saw the few pictures on Czech television, of the Saltires waving at each other in George Square, the seas of YES. My stomach tensed. I'd had the same sensation when I read that Section 28 had been repealed or that Scotland would have marriage equality. It all felt so far away, in a place I didn't recognise.

I sat up all night following the referendum results online with a sore feeling in my belly. When it was over I spent hours on my bed, deflated, angry, and yet somehow confirmed in my prejudice.

'I'm not the best person to ask,' I said to Lev. 'I've been away too long.'

He told me he'd signed up for a talk on Scottish literature after the Enlightenment by a visiting lecturer at the university. 'Maybe we can go together?'

'Sure. Okay, sure.'

I went to Foyles and bought him books by Muriel Spark and James Hogg. I downloaded *Trainspotting* and *Shallow Grave* for us to watch. He turned the books over in his hand. 'This is all Scotland?'

His brows came together, and I was smitten.

I wake to my mother peering down through her massive specs. It takes a moment to get my bearings. She's touching me just above the elbow. I think she might have prodded me awake.

'I've got an appointment in half an hour,' she says. 'Got to get going.'

'What time is it?'

'Near enough nine-thirty.'

'Why didn't you wake me?'

I sit up, my thoughts clarifying. I'd had an idea that there would at least be time for us to sit and have breakfast together. She's turning over her car keys in her hand.

'Maybe see you next time you're up?'

'Mum, you can come down to visit any time.'

'I take it you won't be back for Christmas.'

'I... don't know.'

'Niall's coming for Christmas.'

For as long as I can remember, Christmas has been a potluck gathering with my family of the moment. Strongly flavoured food, chatter, maybe some impromptu music and dancing. No presents, just presence. And not a bauble in sight.

'Come and stay. For as long as you like, any time.'

She murmurs something as she moves away from the bed.

'You'll come? We could go to Kew Gardens.'

'Listen, don't forget anything.'

'You'll come?'

'Well, yes, yes. If you're sure you're okay with your old mum cramping your style.'

It's raining again, so I take my time packing. I hesitate before dropping *Sleeping Murder* into my bag, partly because I can't remember whodunit, and partly as a souvenir.

I've heard it said that a person's true home is the one they grew up in and the rest is just playing houses. Maybe I'm ready to come back. Called back to the mother ship. It happened to my mother, after all.

It wouldn't cross her mind that I might want to stay longer. She's known me in these years as a leave-taker, a runner. It's what I do. I knew from an early age that I would depart on the first passing cyclone.

Still, might there not be some part of her that would be pleased if I told her I wanted to come home?

Davie

Princes Street's a mouth full of broken teeth. Makes me ashamed in a way. Starbucks, Maccy D's, Primark. Could be any high street anywhere if it weren't for the shops selling shortbread and See You Jimmy hats. Loads of empty storefronts. World Heritage Site my arse.

Least the weather makes sense. Wind lifts the tufties on Jordan's head. He puts his arms out, makes giant steps towards the pedestrian crossing, sleeves of his nice coat blowing out huge. Me, I'm huddled up in my jacket, desperate to get out the cold.

He watches a tram rounding the corner from St Andrew Square in slow-mo and the sight of it makes him blink with surprise.

'Have you not been on one yet?' he says, jaw dangling when I say no, and so we end up running for the stop, rootling around for change then gliding a few stops.

I can't stop myself from going near his shoulder and breathing in while he gazes out. He's all cola and cake this one, like a big kid.

Walk back under shop awnings. Christmas is just everywhere. Late-night openings, folk at the shows in the glowing gardens. Jordan stops to admire the lights, like it's exotic to him after all those years away, and of course I'm bah humbug about the whole business.

Our destination's an American-style diner he remembers on Elm Row, so we take a left, heading downhill.

'We went there for my birthday once,' he says. 'The waiters brought out a cupcake with a sparkler on it and my mum had a coronary because she thought they were going to charge extra.' He scans the signs. 'I could've sworn it was around here somewhere.'

We decide his restaurant has been replaced by this fancy chrome-fronted café-bistro. We have to stand at the edge of the pavement to make out the name stretched along the window. E-L-E-M-E-N-T.

It's empty save for the twink in regulation polo behind the counter. White-blonde hair, tons of piercings. Well, it's a look. I'm wondering for a moment how I know him, and then it comes. Messy night in CC's tail-end of the summer, a trample over Calton Hill, a tenement stair. He was Rob or Andrew or James or Scott. He'd said his name on the dance floor, but I hadn't caught it.

'Table for two?'

What really stuck was how quickly he undid my shirt using the fingers of one hand. Afterwards, he fired up a doobie, and we sat up in bed passing it back and forth until we were baked silly. I'm not saying I'm proud of myself.

Twink's pushing back his hair to get a better look at us. I squirm a bit, but nah, he's looking with friendly expectancy, like he would any passing trade.

Jordan picks a table by the window, and we order pasta, nothing too garlicky, and drinks: a half carafe of red for me, which I change to a glass when Jordan asks for a ginger beer. I notice the appreciative look that Rob or Andrew or James or Scott gives Jordan when he hands back the wee card with the specials on it.

What do we look like to him, I'm wondering. Couple of old pals? Second date? He hovers at Jordan's side as he scratches out the order.

The furthest corner of the window's the usual fresco of posters pushing Polish-Scottish get-togethers, stuff happening in the youth hostel, last year's festival shows. Never used to be restaurants in this part of town with board games piled at the end of the bar and wee nooks with couches and coffee tables, but now they're everywhere.

'Quiet, isn't it?'

He's whispering. It's the London thing, he's used to noise. He's leaning forward with his hands on the table while peering around. Fingertips close enough for me to touch.

It's different, sitting across from him like this. For the first time I get a look at his face square on. Piercing boy's right: he *is* nice to look at. Eyelids that crank slowly upwards when he's in mid-flow. Straining to get all the way over those baby blues.

'I like your hair,' he says.

'Got it done this morning.'

'It really suits you.'

First haircut in ages. I felt a right baldy when I left the salon. I'd spent a good hour traipsing Broughton Street, not really feeling it. The bell tinkled and straight away my ears started thumping with all the music and chatter and hairdryers going. My first instinct was to retreat but Alison spotted me in the mirror over someone's cottony head and frilled her fingers. She had a cancellation in ten if I didn't mind waiting.

Tried not to look when she sat us in front of the mirror. She ran her hand back and forth through my hair, funnelling the curls higher. The press of her fingers against my scalp was a narcotic. Tried to hold myself upright in the chair while she sprayed and scissored.

She asked after Frank, dropped in his name like it was nothing, and it twigged that I hadn't so much as thought about him that whole morning. 'Oh, you know Frank,' was all I said. No doubt she had a pile of questions, but I wasn't about to go into all that. She took the hint. Spoke about her kids, their Christmas lists, her training for the Women's 10K. I smiled and nodded along, and the weight slowly came off the top of my head.

At the till, Alison closed a hand over my wallet.

'Listen, don't be a stranger, darling.'

Her face was kind. I've near burned through the last of this month's rent money, so it was a big phew from me. I managed to hold it together until I was back out on the street. Some effort. By the time I got to Bellevue I was heaving out the sobs. Didn't care who saw me out their big, fuck-off windows.

When I'd dried up, I took a selfie and sent it to Carol.

Check you, Haircut 100, she texted back.

But what I wanted was a real proper hug.

Anyway, Rob or James or whatever lowers a basket onto the table. Jordan tears his bread into wee bits, eventually popping a crumb into his mouth, which he then chews round and round like it's gum. He asks me if I've seen this or that film. He runs me through the plot of one of his favourite movies, about two actors getting pished and up to no good in the countryside in the sixties, and then has an eppie when I say I've not even heard of it.

I find myself laughing it off, quite content to sit and listen. But he looks at me, his mouth still working, needing me to do something with the silence.

'How was your trip away, then?' I say.

'My mother seems well enough.'

'When'd you last see her?'

'Five years.' Then, when he clocks the look on my face: 'Oh, we're like that, my family. We've... no hold over each other.'

He keeps nodding, even as he's looking away, looking back, dropping his eyes.

Our drinks land on the table. Another admiring look at Jordan from you-know-who, and I'm like, do I even exist here?

Jordan asks about my parents.

'My old... dad lives over in Portrush. Northern Ireland. Nothing much to say. Him and his wife spend their lives on the golf course.'

The old boy sent a card after I'd texted about me and Frank, with flowers and butterflies on the front and deepest sympathies inside. Made me laugh in a way. Then he phoned to say he would've come over if he could. He and Lucille were going on holiday, Sharm El-Sheikh, and they'd lose their deposit if they cancelled.

'Dad, naebody died.' I managed to keep it light. We might have been rearranging a quick pint. 'Course, you must have your holiday!'

'I was... I liked Frank,' he said. 'You know how I liked him, David, but this holiday's been booked for months. You know how hard it is for Lucille to get time off work.' He lowered his voice. 'She'll go nuts if she doesn't get her holiday.'

I've taken a couple of trips on the pocket rocket in the years since they upped sticks. But they've recently moved again, downsizing. Now, whenever he phones, I have to invent in my head the room or hallway he's calling from. And sometimes when I phone him and he asks how I am and what's what, and all that phoney stuff, I have this urge to say, 'Dad, you know what, I'm *sad*,' though I never do.

'I mean, we get on fine,' I say to Jordan. 'He knows where I am. I know where he is. We're not in each other's pockets.'

Truth is, we're alike, the old boy and me. I can see that now. I've got his crazy hair and his way of folding his arms across his chest when he's not sure of something.

Big difference is I'd cry at the news. *Greetin Teenie*. It was affectionate, I think. 'You're all heart,' he'd sometimes say, real quiet. 'You'd cry at anything.' Maybe my mum was the same. Maybe that's why it's okay by him.

Now I'm wondering if he's still got that photo of me on display next to Lucille's gallery of toothless grandkids. The one where my hair runs in dribbles down the side of my face and I'm looking like I want to lamp the photographer.

Jordan's looking at me, nodding. He's got this way of looking and nodding that makes me feel like I'm expected to keep talking. It's the counsellor all over again.

'My da... I mean, I don't have all that many memories of my mum, but I do remember my dad turned very quiet after she died. Not so much depressed, just, it was like he turned himself down, you know? For the rest of his life. Did everything for me, everything was for me, you know, but it was all sort of... shite. Like life went into grey. You know?'

Did I say all that out loud?

My face is hot. I tuck my hands under my oxters.

On the other side of the table Jordan takes a swig of ginger beer, too fast, and an ice-cube collides with his front teeth.

'Oh, serves me right...'

I scrabble for his napkin and lean over to wipe, not wanting him to mess up his swanky shirt. He puts a hand over mine, meaning to take the napkin off me, and for a wee minute, before Rob or Andrew or James or Scott appears with the food, we sit there with me holding his hand in full view of the street. Not saying anything. Just smiling and looking just past each other.

Course, my brain's doing its dinger.

In that moment of nearly tipping juice down his front, he looked so... young, and I just wanted to say, look, I'm sorry. I'm sorry I was one of the ones that hurt you.

Christ.

We both notice the length of the silence at the same exact moment, and then Jordan gives my hand a squeeze and lifts away.

I've forgotten how this is meant to work. Romance. Not that I'm looking.

Courting, the old boy calls it. *Coortin.*

With Frank it was something else. He used to come into the place I worked back when it was The Daily Grind, and we had a CD player behind the counter with the same three discs going round on a constant loop.

I didn't pay him much mind at first but one day he came in by himself and stood around until I had a moment's peace, and then he just leaned over and asked me out.

'Sure, whatever,' I said, my heart going boom in my tin chest.

He had an unbelievably square jaw, like that boy Billy Crudup.

We played pool in the New Town bar that night. Five games, best of five, and I won every last one of them. Cleaned up at the darts too. Frank had no sense of aim. Gave it big licks, got nowhere, threw his arrows across the table like a diva.

He was fit, though. Handsome. A smoothie. I liked the idea of him out of his shirt.

We went back to his flat in the West Port, and I sat hugging one of the cushions off the sofa while I listened to him chunter on about Chet Baker who jumped out of a window and Billie Holiday, arrested on her deathbed for possessing heroin. He was full of it.

I found I loved the nearness of him. It made me suddenly aware of every bit of my own body.

Back up the Walk we go, me and old Jordan, past empty restaurant windows, the blue-lit chippy, all the Saturday shoppers shivering their way home past folk dressed up for their night out. No rain for once, though the streets are shining bright. Look at me, I feel like saying to the passing people, look at me on a night out with someone who's not Frank.

The fenced-off bit outside CC's is full of fleecy hoods bobbing about with smoke streaming out the front of them, like some weird act at the fringe. Couple of bears cross at the lights and stride past, holding hands. It was at this exact spot, a couple of years back, where Frank and I found ourselves caught up in the aftermath of a bashing and ended up in A&E with some poor kid with a dent in his cheekbone. Frank stepped in without taking a breath. Sent the crowd scattering. It's what he does. He wades into other people's fights and misfortunes, rights their wrongs, then leaves again, like the Terminator tuned to nice mode.

The whole thing made me rage, all these gadgies crowding round a couple of harmless gays, pushing and shoving. There was a time when I would've got stuck in there with the worst of them. Fists, feet, the works. Thing is, I know I've got a temper on me, but I don't like to fight. I do not want to have to fight.

We turn onto Picardy Place, clinging to the curve of the road. Squeeze between the bouncers at the entrance to The Street. For some reason I expected Jordan to be shy, but he brightens as soon as we walk through the door. He pulls himself straight. Crosses the floor in strides. He's home. I catch sight of us in the mirror behind the bar staff: me in my scabby jacket and the new haircut that makes my head look like it's been sharpened. Him buttoned to the neck in his spotless coat. I steady myself against his arm. In the mirror it looks like I'm trying to hide.

'Is it me,' he says when we're settled, 'or is everyone in here twelve?'

I check out a nearby table-load of humans, every one of them deep in confab with their phones. I mind all too well that age, all the fear and lousy chat. Waste of nice hair and cheekbones.

Door bangs behind us and another group blows in, reeking of the cold and straight people's perfume. They shift around then push towards the bar. Lads holding on to their womenfolk for safety.

Jordan's twitching along to the music. Doing his toothy smile.

'I like her voice,' he says. 'Amy Winehouse.'

I've not got the heart to tell him this is Adele's 'Rolling in the Deep'.

'Look at them,' he says, nodding towards the crowd at the bar. 'Refugees from a wedding reception. Imagine them in a place like this ten years ago.'

'I was nineteen first time I went up CC's,' I say. 'Sat in the bus stop half an hour before I went through the door, terrified someone might see us. My dad or one of his mates, someone from school, god. Bouncers used to size you up, check you looked gay enough. No, honest! I got to the bar and panicked and ordered red wine. Barman had to go through and blow the dust off the bottle.'

'We're mainstream now. We've assimilated.' He has to raise his voice to be heard.

'The last time I was here in Edinburgh I saw a headline on one of those placards outside the paper shop on Broughton Street. *Scotland Best in Europe for LGBT Equality.* Something like that. I stood there for ages, just staring at it, more bewildered than anything else, and then I burst into laughter. Anyone walking past would have thought I was having some kind of episode.'

His face stays close to mine. I rub his hand, easing out the cold left by his glass. The music intrudes again, Kylie this time, and we both smile and shimmy a wee bit as we reach for our drinks. Another week and they'll be on to the Christmas tunes. Slade, Elton, all that crap. I can feel his eyes on me, and I let him see my smile before looking away. I can't hold his eye for long. I keep waiting for the moment when he sees me. I mean, *sees* me.

I watch that lot at the bar, their concentrating faces and arms tightly around waists. Jordan gets up and makes a beeline for the bogs.

Must have been third year, so we'd have been fourteen or fifteen. I mean, we were kids, you know. Here's how it went. First we got him after the bell, hauled him to the embankment near school. One of us threw an arm lock on him so he couldn't move. Standing

93

at the top of the slope I watched as Hutton toe-punted his bag. It landed down past all the rubbish they dumped down there, right on the edge of the railway line. Everything still and quiet. One of the others was next to me, quite close, mouth-breathing hard enough to see.

My head hurt. My heart going. This was a new game.

And then all the pounding inside was joined by another kind of drumbeat, moving closer. I could see light coming around the bend, searching the ground. Overhead wires buzzed. Hutton was all hunched up, waiting. You could tell when he was excited. It got so he didn't know if it was Tuesday or Christmas.

He'd been at the High a few months, this Hutton. At first, he seemed always to be on his tod, going around the edges of the place, kicking at cans. A rumour went round that he'd got chucked out a school down south for setting fire to the science block. Not that I ever bought into that bullshit. It was a funny name, Hutton Kern. One of those second name first names, like the routine on my dad's Billy Connolly vids. *Crawford, Crawford, where's Farquhar?* Worst of all for Hutton, he was English. The ultimate no-no. There was an undertow of something about him. Experience. Somehow everyone just assumed he was having actual sex all the time, maybe because he was that bit taller and had a bit of stubble. When he walked into the classroom, folk either crossed their arms or did something with their hair.

The way he walked with the shoulders going up and down and his chest high. The deepness of his voice. Something about him. High colour of his skin, the size of his hands. Made me want to be friends with him.

Now he gave a signal, a grunt or a wave. One kick to the arse of the trousers and down went our captive, half running, half stumbling, onto the line.

I felt the weight under my feet as the train rolled closer. Jordan scrambled for his bag and threw himself onto the bank. I screwed my eyes nearly shut. There was a kind of howling sadness inside me that could have just about drowned out the racket of that train.

I almost don't notice when he gets back to the table.

'You were miles away,' he says.

'Sorry. Dreaming...'

Maybe we didn't do this to Jordan, but he's the one I see when I go back over that whole episode in my head.

Now I've got this need to ask him, a need to remember properly and also to explain, really get into it.

And at the same time, every time I think about it, it ends up making me want to crawl away and disappear.

Another round from the bar. Jordan hands me my voddy and looks down into his cranberry juice with a face like insults.

'Veggie *and* teetotal,' I say. 'Give that man a halo.'

He smiles.

'You never touch the stuff?'

'Allergic.'

'Like, spots and sneezing and throwing up?'

'I was never much of a drinker. I just never... had the taste for it.'

'Right, well, chink-chink.'

'Cheerio.'

We're both laughing, but there's a tightness to his smile. A couple of times when I lift up my drink I catch him throwing funny looks at my glass like it's his rival for my attention.

Bell goes for last orders, and we get caught in the convoy heading over to CC's.

Jordan looks put out at the thought of us cutting our losses.

'Come on,' I say, feeling a sudden burst of inner sunshine, steering him to the back of the line.

'This used to be such a *grubby* place,' he says when we're inside, trailing his fingers along the exposed brickwork like he expects it to crumble.

'It was a fucking midden.'

'Look at that now. You could eat your bar snacks off that floor. And feel...' He lifts his feet.

'Aye, no more sticky floors.'

Basement's a sauna. Faces I recognise, everywhere. As I nudge my way forward, this boy leaning against the archway that separates the bar from the dance floor clocks me, then turns and whispers behind his hand to one of his pals. He's in one of those suits that looks like jammies. I send over a quick nod, but his name won't come.

Friends of Frank's. There's no hiding. It's been the same story for eighteen years. A quick trip to the shops was always a human obstacle course. *Oh, there's so-and-so, I'd better just say hello.* Like it was a chore. The ones he didn't know would keek over, scan his narrow body, catching my dirty look before moving past.

'You thirsty?' I shout. 'I'll get us a couple of waters?'

'Sure.'

So I join the rammy while Jordan hovers nearby, looking fine in his leaf-print shirt, most of his attention on the dance floor. I get to the front, yell my order over the taps and collect our bottles, turning to shoulder-charge my way through the scrum.

We perch among coats and jumpers. Shelf at my elbow's covered with empties. DJ's playing this insane mash-up of Gaga and some punk thing. We watch the dancers and Jordan kills himself at the sight of this kid in a checked shirt with most of his hair shaved apart from a wee curl at the front, pogoing up and down.

Blurred Faces

Jordan nods towards the guy.

'If I didn't feel like an old man before...'

'I mind a time when I knew the name of every single person in this place.'

Lights flash in diagonals across bodies. I head for the bogs and get lost in a sweet-smelling cloud that's hissing out from somewhere on the other side of the floor. Muscle queen with a brick of a head smiles and bows his head and makes this big show of letting me pass, sweeping his arms around like I'm *the* Queen and he's one of my minions. I turn and offer my most regal smile. Honestly, I'm feeling pretty happy.

The moving figures start to blur and lose their edges. Shapes drift through the fog like ghosts. When I get back from the bar Pyjama Man and his mate are sitting on the other side of the dance floor, gawping over at Jordan. What are their names? I'm past caring. The world and their fuck buddy could see me out and about with someone who's not Frank, and I wouldn't care.

Pyjama Man catches me looking and mouths words, pointing at Jordan. Jordan turns to me, eyebrows rising.

'Oh, that's... folk I know,' I say. 'They're more friends of... They're friends of my ex – you know. *Were.*'

I raise a hand and give what I hope looks a contented smile. I'm feeling kind of contented, actually. Frank's pals wave back but they're not for moving. They're not interested in me, not really. I just pretend they're not there. What I want, the absolute cherry on today's cake, would be for my crew to walk in. Dan, Luca, Carol, Evie. Our own wee circle on the dance floor, taking turns in the middle and busting our moves. We haven't done that for a long time. I imagine them saying nice things about Jordan.

'Come on,' I say. 'Time to dance.'

He sticks up his hands in protest, saying something about his bad knee, but I'm feeling daft enough to insist on getting him up on his feet.

And, oh my god, state of his moves, like Crazylegs Crane on acid. I grab him by the hands and try to bend him into the right groove, but he seems in the zone, so I let him be, meet him where he is.

Madonna comes on, 'Papa Don't Preach', and the floor fills, and I feel straight up free. Jordan tips his head back, shakes his head so hard I'm scared he'll do himself a mischief.

We make it all the way to time, and as we trot down the road, I can feel him damp and shiny beside me. I try my very damnedest to walk in a straight line.

'It's a while since I moved like that,' he says.

He rattles on, going back over the things we've seen, listing the tracks they played, some of it our vintage, some of it way fast for our rattling joints, the way the floor turned slippery under our feet, everyone getting sweaty, even though it's November and freezing.

He's sober, but he's flying.

We keep going, turning at the Pilrig Church, and somewhere Jordan notices that I'm away with the fairies and only half listening.

'You know... I wish...'

He doesn't say what he wishes.

'You're a lucky boy,' I say after a moment. 'You get to go back to London day after tomorrow. London, fuck's sake.'

'No, you're right,' he says. 'You're right. I mean... What I'm saying is, it was nice to meet up again.'

'It's been a laugh, hasn't it? It's been fun.'

'Right. I mean... I'll remember this.'

I can feel him, warm beside me. As we move down the road I find myself telling him I'm thinking of taking a trip myself, to Portrush to see my old boy, maybe in the new year. It was half a thought till now. Saying it makes it more likely I'll actually go.

'How long will you be away?'

'Knowing my old boy, not long.'

He laughs and reaches a hand, just misses as I take a wee totter over a loose slab. I turn, meaning to connect, but just then there's a shout from somewhere off to our right, a clatter of cans. Crowd of kids clustered just inside the entrance to the park. Course they're high as kites. One of the boys is enacting some major drama, waggling his arms around above his head.

As I watch, this kid swivels in our direction. Slowly, sort of like a signal has sounded, his pals follow suit, until the whole group's facing us.

'Oh, it's like that scene out of *The Birds*,' Jordan mutters.

A couple of the kids break loose. They don't come far, just towards the gates of the park, but I can feel Jordan stiffen beside me.

Fuckin poofs!

Aye, fuckin bufties!

'It's just kids,' I say, but I can feel the rage starting inside me.

One of them growls like a dog and the others start up, fucking howling at the moon.

I don't want to fight.

'It's not like they own the road,' I say, and he murmurs agreement, but there's something about him that isn't sure, the way he's dipped just behind me, and his fear's making me want to protect him, or better still, turn and face down these wankers, blast the wee bastards away with my dragon breath.

I feel my body squaring solid, every part of my core tightening. I don't recognise the roar that comes out of me.

'Fuck off, you bunch of wee fannies.'

A few of them totter out onto the road. Their hilarity pursues us down the street, but they don't come any closer. We walk together, at a clip, just about intact.

'My hero,' Jordan says, all out of breath. Me, I'm buzzing all over with adrenaline. We're all the way to the next block before I realise I've got my hand in his, sort of pulling him along.

I don't think we ever held hands in the street, me and Frank. Not once.

First time for everything.

He's miles away now. Safe as houses. I keep watch. His head shakes a couple of times in disagreement with someone I can't see.

I flunked saying anything. I mean, I felt bold for a minute, and maybe it was just the bevvy talking, but I honestly thought it was all going to come out. I had this need to confess, same way I sometimes feel the need to dig my nails into my palm.

Lying there, still buzzed from the night, I got in fast towards the subject.

'Bunch of cunts at that place, though.'

I felt him bristle.

'Sorry. Cursing.'

'It's not that. School. I don't care to think about it anymore.'

'Well, they gave you a hard time, didn't they? Hutton Kern and that lot?'

'Well, I'm an adult now, David. I'm not that… bullied kid anymore.'

'Sure, but…'

'Hutton Kern? Are you making that up?'

'No kidding. He was a clown.'

'You…' His voice hesitated, even as I could sense his body tensing. 'You remember a lot,' he said.

'Suppose.'

'I mean, you obviously have a good memory.'

'Well…'

Then radio silence, not like him at all. I was aware of our knees and shoulders touching, and I really wanted to move closer, but I was also scared.

'Do you remember…?' He cleared his throat. 'Do you remember what I was like?'

'Well, look, you were—'

'Because it's all a blur to me now. I can't remember if I was kind, I can't remember if I was smart. I can't remember if I was daft. Was I daft? Did I draw attention to myself?'

'No, I... I didn't know you all that well, but you seemed... nice, you were cool...'

'Come on...'

'No, but what I'm saying is... Sure, you had a hard time of it, but I... My feeling was, you'd be okay. Another thing, you were deep down your own man.' I wriggled around, feeling pinned, hemmed in. 'Honestly, I was a bit jealous of you. I think I would have liked to be pals with you.'

More silence. I wasn't much enjoying this moment, and then it came to me that, of course, he didn't want to go back over any of this. Far as he was concerned, this was ancient history, nothing to do with us.

But still I went on, like a wee dog with a bone.

'Sorry, shouldn't have brought that up. I'm just saying, it was rough.'

Silence.

'I mean, what would you do if... if you saw any of that lot again?'

I was sweating, edgy as hell.

'I'd obviously want to rub their noses in how well I'm doing, how great I look!'

He laughed, not a very convincing laugh, and I tried to laugh, too, but I was shivering, and not with the cold.

'I suppose,' he said, 'that what I'd really like to do is to go back there with the head I've got now, all my... wisdom, confidence. Charisma. I'd swagger through them, face them down. I'd be Clint Eastwood. I'd be Bruce Lee.'

He grinned. 'No. I'd be Lauren Bacall. Barbara Stanwick. Tuesday Weld. Angie Dickinson.'

He laughed to himself, and suddenly I felt... *lonely*. It's a mad feeling, to be in bed next to someone, and lonely.

'Thing is,' he said, 'even if I could go back in time, you know what, I'd still run from them. If I think about school, I'm that fourteen-year-old boy again. So yeah, I'd just run.'

The silence he'll leave behind. Part of me wants the morning to come soon as, so we get it over and done with – all that going on to our Instas and accepting each other's follow requests and saying we'll keep in touch. Fuck that.

Maybe I'll surprise myself. Enjoy the silence. There was a time when I thought I wanted nothing more than to have this place to myself.

The old boy used to pretend surprise when he came home and found me watching telly.

'You still here, are you? Still hanging around making the place look untidy?'

We went back to our separate ends, the pair of us, and came together in the late evening for a cuppy and a bit of toast and *Prisoner*. The one thing we could just about agree on, a ten-year-old Ozzie soap. I tried to sit through his football. At school I'd learned just enough chucking the ball around to be able to pass comment. I even knew the offside rule, but I couldn't make myself care. Formula One I found pointless, like watching folk with more cash than me have fun at the shows.

What I really wanted out of him was the story of how he met my mum. I wasn't going to push. I knew it was hard for him to open up, and I didn't want him thinking it was worrying me. I mean, I'd gotten the basics over the years. How she'd been at the uni on an exchange thing, and how they'd met on the randan, and when she went back to Spain they'd kept in touch and travelled back and forth.

Another thing, I knew they'd married young, and I know they were happy. I mean, in all the photos they're looking at each other and they seem just really happy.

If I have a wish it's to hear the story in my dad's words. I want him to tell me what my mum was like. I mean, what she meant to him, and if he sees anything of her in me. I still want that. I want that whole story.

Weird, I still mind the look the old boy gave us when I told him I'd finally be moving out at the ripe old age of twenty-four. This was after him giving out at us over and over that he'd left home at sixteen and it never did him any harm and all that when-I-were-a-lad stuff, but when it came to the moment of me actually fucking off he looked stunned.

I told him I had everything all planned out, and he nodded slowly and offered to help me with my stuff.

'No need,' I said. 'My flatmate's going to give me a hand.'

'Your flatmate?'

'Frank.'

Frank, Frank, Frank.

Now I think when we met, I wasn't a complete person. I mean, he had ten years on me, he'd been all over. All I had to bring to the party was darts, frothy coffees, a prize from school for short stories, Kim Wilde. *Prisoner: Cell Block H.* I had all my stretching before me.

Frank was the one in charge, I can see that now: he decided on everything. He kept the bills in a file and went through them with his sharpies at the end of the month. When the washing machine started to stink, or the boiler leaked he wouldn't stop to think – he just rolled up his sleeves and in he went.

He told me about the places he'd visited, and I lapped it all up. Even sat in the library on my lunch breaks: I'd look at pictures of

India, the Middle East and Central America, until I felt like I could sort of relate or at least keep up. It was a way of getting close to him and I suppose a way of widening my horizons. In theory, I wanted more out of my life. I wanted him to show me a bit of life. But what can I say, I'm the world's biggest scaredy-cat.

He didn't do lovey-dovey, Frank. So, I made a joke of it. Big eyes, head on the side. I couldn't quite believe he loved me in the same mental way I loved him.

The main thing, though, was that I wanted to learn from Frank in a way I'd never wanted to learn from my old boy or any of my rakes of teachers. Now I think I ended up doing a copycat thing, a crappy tribute act. I'd surprise him with meals I'd cooked, having carefully followed every step from the book. He ate like a champ, my quiche Lorraine, pasta puttanesca, pea and mint risotto. Nothing turned out quite the way it was meant to – it went claggy in the mouth, or it got stuck to the pan.

He made plans for the places we lived, and I chipped in when we went round IKEA. When he noticed I didn't have any *actual* hobbies of my own, he started to nag me a bit. What are you good at, he wanted to know. What are you into?

I'm into you.

I picked up a notebook and started on a load of stories, about gangsters and the polis and drugs, stuff I knew nothing about. I was always great at starting, less good at finishing.

Just write about yourself, Frank said, which I thought sounded completely nuts.

He used to say there was another side to him. A downside, or a downer side. At first I wasn't sure if he was for real, but then I started to notice the way his smile would stick at the end of a night out. He'd sit in the taxi on the way home with his eyes shut. I knew his work, the interviews, the bantz, the whole routine of being the only gay in an office of booze hounds could get old, but he tried not to bring all that home with him. Mostly, it stayed in the shed when he locked away his bike at the end of the day.

He'd joked for years that news was recession-proof, but when Covid came the papers he worked for lost a ton. Frank watched names disappearing off pages like they were written in invisible ink. He was confined to quarters, the pond went dry, not that there was any conversation with me about it, not really. He turned to copywriting, advertising, soul-destroying stuff, finishing jobs then sitting around waiting for his phone to go.

Wasn't good for him. When he woke in the night, scrambling for a bit of paper and a pen, it made me scared.

'It's a good job you're still gainfully employed,' he said, watching me tug on my big coat, late for my shift delivering groceries. His voice sounded funny, and there was something fake about his smile.

Everything got worse then, which meant more cuts, the copywriting work drying up. He stopped sharing his thoughts with me. He didn't think I was ready.

He was right, I wasn't ready. I was a kid. My shoulders were not broad.

And then he took a holiday from himself, which meant sitting down on the couch and staying there for ages, watching the box in his PJs. This Frank who hated being still, who stopped for nobody, who ran three times a week and cycled to work in all weathers. I'd never seen him so slumped, staring like he was hypnotised.

The house went to shit. The mail – all of it addressed to him – collected on the table, the dust gathered, and after a while I went down the hole after him. Couldn't help it. I always had to do what he did. So, there we were, squashed together on the couch. Sad, slouched. Hiding in the noise of *Homes Under the Hammer* and *The One Show*, eating along to *Bake-Off*.

Everything can change in a minute.

I keep going back in my head to that day, three, four years ago, when Frank was somewhere in the middle of his wobble or dip or whatever he ended up calling it.

It was a Saturday, a rare day off for me. We'd lain in the scratcher all morning and so far Frank was showing no signs of moving. Down in the kitchen, hunting for something to eat, I heard a soft kind of thump from the other end of the house. The coat rack, along with all the coats and bags and hats and gloves and all other random shit had fallen off the wall. The whole lot was lying in a heap at the bottom of the stairs.

I went barefoot up the stairs.

'I know, I'll be up in a minute,' he said, but he didn't move.

When I told him the coat rack had come down, he shook his head. 'Davie, I'll do something about it later.'

The way he looked at me then, it was like a cold wave came off him.

When I got back from my work, Frank was up, and I could hear the shower going. It was something at least. The heap was still there at the bottom of the stairs. The mess of coats and bags looked like something about to clump together and come to life, shouting the odds.

My dad was handy. He used to fix everything no bother. How come I ended up useless? I knew where the toolbox lived, the spirit level and the drill. Surely there was some splinter of the old boy's ability in my DNA.

I dragged the old stepladder to the bottom of the stairs. I might even do this, I was thinking. After a half hour of measuring and marking and banging nails, I stood back. There it was, the coat rack, once again fixed to the wall.

And it was squint.

Not massively, but enough that you would see if you were looking. Frank would notice; the old boy would have noticed. It went through my mind to cut my losses and pile the coats back up onto their hooks, letting them dangle at that funny angle. Then Frank came to me again, his face when he looked at me, all empty. I climbed up and took out the screws. Slid the rack a half inch higher at one side. Nailed the bastard in place.

It was a start. I'd screwed a piece of wood onto a wall, for god's sake, but it felt like I'd built a door. When Frank came downstairs I'd show off. For now, I wanted to stare at the perfectly straight coat rack on the wall and just enjoy it, like it was a work of art.

And that was the start of something. For the both of us. A day later Frank sat at the dinner table in his PJs and jumper and ate a meal I'd made for him, not exactly what you'd call a banquet, but something that passed muster. I made a playlist and blasted it through the house. Coaxed him out of bed the day after that and took him for a long walk.

We visited our pals Brian and George and sat in their garden, and he laughed for the first time in ages, taking control of their Spotify and lining up his favourites, ripping the pish out of their taste, letting them know that when we first met I'd thought Buckingham Nicks was one really posh person.

I held him that night. I mean, we really held on to each other like we meant it.

He was done with papers, he said. So he got out his laptop and started talking about the things he'd wanted to do with his life but never got round to trying. A bookshop chain came back to him. He'd always loved reading and thought he would shine in a job that involved books and people. The only problem was the online interview, which lasted a whole day.

'I'm in my fifties,' he said. 'Either they want me for their damned shop, or they don't.'

After lockdown he got on the shortlist for a job as a fundraiser with a human rights charity. This was his calling. This was what he'd been put on the earth to do. He was all flushed and excited. But then the interview turned out to be another pisser. His oppos for the job were all young and posh and bouncy. His words. Frank lasted as long as the splitting into groups stage before cutting his losses.

He said he would go back to the uni and learn a new skill. He'd be a teacher. After watching a thing on telly about middle-class plumbers, he decided he would get trained up, start his own business. There's money in pipes, he said, looking at me with a kind of pleading smile that just about wrecked me.

'What's gotten into you, anyway?'

He lobbed the question across the room. Maybe he'd seen me trying, putting myself about the place, sorting through bills, recipes, tidying, straightening everything out.

'Dunno what you mean.'

He shrugged, turned to the side and I could see the outline of something, a kind of confusion in the deep groove of his jaw. Made me scared in a way. I wanted him, but I wanted the Frank of before. I wanted him to put one of his great hands on my arm and tell me that everything was fine, and that he'd take care of everything.

He was improving. There were signs. A wee grin here, a bout of frenzied internet surfing there. He sat up most of one night staring into space and the next day he showered, dressed, unchained his bike and went on a tour around his old workplaces, reminding everyone he was still alive. That night he cooked, and we drank this ridiculously overpriced red from Villeneuve's. We chatted about his day across the table as though nothing had happened, picking up where we'd left off months earlier, even though I knew there was change. It was in him, and it was in me. I'd seen what it might be like to be my own person, separate from him, and that made me scared. The old me was gone.

I kept myself busy, taking on extra shifts at the café, enjoying my promotion, the praise the boss gave us, walking the long route home. Energy levels through the roof, no kidding. In the flat, I found jobs to do, stuff to keep my hands busy. I poured out loving words and I took him to bed and clung on, but I couldn't always look him in the eye.

Jordan's sleeping in that child way, sucking in air then gasping it out like he's been holding his breath for a game. Wish I could sleep like that. Sometimes he squirms, moves his head, eyelids quivering but never fully opening, and I stay frozen until he settles again.

If he wakes up and sees me, I mean, *recognises* me, what then? Knowing me I'll deny it. *No, no, no,* I'll say, rat-a-tat. I'm the worst liar you've ever seen. He'll know in an instant that I'm fucking lying. I don't want to lie. I want to show myself in full and then disappear. I mean, just completely disappear like something in a story.

Love me?

One day I heard myself say it, and it sounded wrong, not cute at all. Nails down a blackboard time. It was only a moment, but Frank had heard, and he'd seen. He became all hard-eyed and stared into his coffee, and then when he lifted his head he gave this look, like he had words to say but he couldn't manage to say them.

And my heart cracked. I mean, I could actually hear it breaking all the way across.

'I really love you.'

And I meant it. I loved him. It was just that everything was different.

*

Anyway, we kept on for a while like nothing had happened. We were okay. There'd been a thing, this change and we'd come through. Went back to our life, separately and together. Worked and went to gigs and walked around and saw our pals and took turns at the cooker. I loved him. We were different now, different people, but that was okay.

But Frank had other ideas. And there were moments in the time that followed – before he told me what he wanted, and how his life was going to be – when I would say I still loved him, and I saw him looking back at me without saying anything, and *it's not enough* was what I heard in my head. *You're not enough.*

Jordan

We fall into bed, complaining about the cold like it's a fickle friend. There's some whispered chat as we cling for warmth. We're still going back over the night we've had as he lies on top of me, and I marvel again at the slightness of him naked. We laugh especially hard when he tries to emulate my clumsy dance moves under the covers. I put a hand to my chest, feigning offence.

Then: 'Go to sleep, Jordan. No, come on. I need to sleep.'

He turns away, onto his side. I try to reach around, but he's unresponsive. He pulls his legs to his chest and mutters a pointed goodnight, so I huddle, the laughter softly falling away, my head whirling towards some kind of night, and the next thing I'm aware, the light's squeezing around the edges of the curtains.

'You okay?'

He's bleary, his hair pummelled.

'That was fun last night.'

'It was decent,' he says.

He gets up to pee, and as soon as he returns, almost with the closing of the door, it becomes obvious that something has changed. His face is a gracious mask, and his offer of coffee is almost formal, as though I'm meeting this tousled nude man for the first time.

I think there has been a misunderstanding...

It's only when we're kneeling on the mattress facing each other that his face softens. He sighs like he's got nothing better to do, and he puts his hands on me, but in an efficient rather than a tender way. I lean over to kiss him, he leans away, but we shift to fit, and soon enough he's putting me inside him, easing backwards, stretching out his arms to steady himself, his eyes on something just over my shoulder.

'What you up to today?' he asks.

Stress on the you. Not that there was ever we or us, not in any meaningful sense, but the question is stuck on the end of a sigh that makes me think he's just going through the motions now. I say something about spending the afternoon with my brother, helping him get the flat ready. My niece is coming. I give a little lift of the eyebrows to show that this is the main event, a real cause for celebration. Everything else, including him, is lather.

He pulls the curtain, looking out at the haze, and as he lets the folds swing back into place I come to a decision: no sense in drawing this out. I get out of bed and step into my underwear with as much dignity as I can manage on a gammy knee. I pull on my shirt with my back turned to him, and a minute later I'm up and hovering by the door.

Still, there's something unresolved, and from the look David's giving me he's actually a little surprised at my hurry.

'You know: if you're ever down south,' I say.

'I've got your number.'

'I'm not heading off till tomorrow. Maybe we could grab a farewell drink?'

'Sounds good.'

I stare downwards. The floorboards are covered with lint from where his socks have moulted.

'David, I know we're… I know you're not ready.'

'Jordan…'

'Your breakup…'

He looks out the window. He almost looks like he might cry.
I think there has been a misunderstanding.
'You're right, I don't know anything. I'm sorry.'
He lifts his head, looks not at me, but past me, towards the door I'll be leaving through.
'Right, well, I'll be seeing you.'
'Yeah. Absolutely. That drink.'

As I take to the stairs, I cling to the railing and the notion that I really could see him again if that's what I want. I could take out my phone and push his number right this very minute. I'd probably hear his phone ringing faintly through the wall.

I keep moving. It's what I do.

I walk back along the Water of Leith. When I was growing up, this part of town was forbidden – full of druggies according to my father – but now everything's changed. My route takes me past the Bonds, a couple of old sugar warehouses that have been converted into flats. There's a sign rising up one of them showing a happy hetero couple, a toddler smiling in the man's huge arms: *The perfect starter family home.* A snip at £350,000.

It's dry for once and the haar's starting to burn away. There's a group of gulls in my path, stamping around, looking for scraps with a greedy sense of entitlement. Me, I'm stuck on David, the image of him saying goodbye without saying anything. The charcoal of his hair complemented the age of his face in a way that was quite beautiful.

I shake my head, trying to move my brain on to the next thought, and of course, Lev's is the face I see next.

Right now, Lev will be on his way to the pool for the early-bird swim session. He'll slam the lengths and then, en route to his shift, he'll stop off at a Georgian-run café called the Silver Table for his morning espresso. Just the single shot: to sharpen him up for the day ahead. Travel, work, travel, class, travel, home, always trying for more.

How long since we last spoke? How long since I last saw him in the canteen or in the corridor between classes and his smile made his face merry?

I get as far as scrolling down to his name before shoving my phone back in my pocket. I wince, picturing the change that went through him that night in the Thai restaurant. *Jordan, I think there has been...*

Lev would answer my call, of course he would. His voice would bounce down the line and I'd be right back at square one.

When I met him, Lev had been in the country three years. He was saving up to move out of his sister's, but it was tough – his part-time job in the care home wasn't all that well-paid. His nephew and niece were growing up, they would be starting school, and he was taking up space that his sister could have turned into an office or a large cupboard.

He worried he would have to move back to Tbilisi.

'If my flat was any bigger...' I said, spreading my hands, mentally shifting around furniture, opening up a corner for him.

The more he talked, the less Lev seemed present in his own life, for all his warmth, his singing and moving in time to the canteen soundtrack. I could see in him a version of myself. He was restless, too, an exile. It was just that I had been running for longer.

I asked him if he ever went out, and he said the bars he'd been to were full of the same faces and there wasn't much variety in the music they played.

'There are people who drink and drink until they cannot stand up,' he said. 'Like back home. It is the same here. People drink to disappear. People drink to hide from who they are.'

He preferred going to gigs and discovering new bands. 'But everything here is just' – he flung out his hands – 'money, money and more money.'

'I'll treat you one of these nights.'

'Oh, you don't ever need to do that,' he said, and he touched my hand.

It was almost nothing, a dab.

He told me he was considering taking up running. Maybe this was something we could do together. I felt elated. And scared. What if he was faster than me? Would he moderate his pace out of kindness so this old man could keep up?

I never once heard him mention a boyfriend. I assumed he didn't have time. We began meeting up more often during the day. He complimented my clothes in a tactile way, and I giggled with delight, and then scolded myself for being silly.

I went home worrying about the language barrier. When he touched my arm and told me he liked my jacket, my hair, what was he saying, really?

The year was ending. There were exams to prep for, papers to mark. I tubed it home at the end of the day with my head falling towards my book. A snatched coffee or chance meeting in the corridor with Lev could leave me energised for the rest of the day.

But sometimes the light that came off him showed up the dingy crooks in my life. My flat felt pokier than ever. If I didn't hear from him or see him at least once a day, a kind of panic set in. I'd dry in class, my mind filled with Lev. One lunchtime while he was queuing, I sneaked a copy of his timetable out of his briefcase and took a photo so I could bump into him in the corridor between classes. At night, I lay awake. Everything would be all right, I told myself. Everything would be fine if he would just want me the way I wanted him.

Looking back, I realise this all sounds a tad melodramatic.

*

At the end of the summer, I surprised him with tickets for Jenny Lee's, a showcase of new bands in Soho. We took the Tube into town after college on the Friday evening. It was the first time we'd been out together, just the two of us. My hair was shorn. I had tried on shirt after gorgeous shirt. On the underground we couldn't talk much because of the train's clatter. We sat with our shoulders and legs touching.

And I was smitten.

I was smitten.

Before the gig I took him for dinner. The restaurant was right across from the venue. Superior Thai it was called. My mouth was dry as we made our way along the street. Part of me knew I was about to do something risky, something that would hurt and probably wreck a friendship, but I couldn't help myself. Our starters arrived and I leaned across the table and told him in my telephone voice that I thought of him as more than a friend and that I thought we clicked, and we should, we should…

At this point I choked, like an underprepared teacher – *we should what?*

He waited with his brows high. Words fell from me onto the table with a wet thud. I thought there was a spark between us, I said. I thought we would work well together.

'I'm saying I think we could… You know… Us… You know…*Us*…'

Half a spring roll, in the grip of a chopstick, was on its way to his mouth.

'Jordan, I think there has been a misunderstanding.'

He was still smiling, but now it looked like a smile of forbearance.

And I saw myself then, or rather I saw the way I must look to him. An older man, whom he liked, very possibly liked very much, but had never considered going to bed with. As I watched him returning with gusto to his food, it came home to me that he was not someone who needed looking after or saving. His solitary journey had made him strong, self-contained.

When I realised how badly I had got it wrong I pushed back my chair and made a dash for the gents, cowered in a cubicle and hid my face in my hands.

Fuck. Fuck. Fuck.

And then we had to sit together in that dark basement, Lev and me, nodding along to a succession of songs with really quite insipid lyrics. Lev's eyes were shining. I could see his energy, his youth and assertiveness in his smile. He would age; he would lose his beauty and maybe at some point that thought would console me, but right now, I was in a shocked state, the precursor to the first stage of grief.

I had offered him a drink and he had wrinkled his nose and said, 'Coke Zero?', not really caring, and I thought: you're so *pure*. How can you be so pure? As I waited at the bar my insides were cringing at what had happened, but seemingly the whole episode had already run off Lev like water.

Towards the end, when the whole place got to its feet, I stayed in my seat, tapping my can of cola, watching the room erupt, praying Lev wouldn't cajole me into strutting my galumphing stuff.

We walked to the underground together. It was a warm evening with just enough of a breeze to cool us off and Lev had taken off his jacket and tied it around his waist. He was giddy from the evening, and as we walked, he went back over the acts we'd seen, in particular a band with a female singer accompanied by a pianist who had performed a mix of French *chansons* and songs by Nick Cave and Tom Waits. Red-lit, they had changed the atmosphere in the room, turning it into a scene from a David Lynch film.

We stopped for a moment in the swaying huddle outside the underground. As I stood there with my arms loose at my sides, Lev turned to face me.

'Thank you, Jordan. It was the perfect night. You have no idea.'

He put his arms around me then pulled away, grinning. He attached himself to the swarm descending the escalator, hand tapping the railing, no doubt in time to one of the tunes still playing in his head.

I stared at his back, not wanting to lose sight, craning my neck upwards as the underground swallowed him.

I would go back now to a different world. An everyday place, where I would have to face myself. I'd sit in my flat that wasn't a home and mark exams and then I would read and listen to podcasts and look online for clothes and sex, always in the hope that in among all those words and pretty pictures there might be something that would tell me what I was supposed to do next, how to travel hopefully and where to look for the next possible Oz.

On the way home that night, a crowd of lads, pressed together in a block, gave me dog's abuse. *Queer*, *poof*, all the classics. I lowered my head as I always do and pushed through.

Davie

Room's blank with daylight. As I strip the bed my head's all Jordan, the way his shape changed when he got naked. Embarrassed about the soft bits, not that I could give a flying fuck. He must be about the same height as Frank, give or take, but a different silhouette. I have to stop myself lying down on the bed and closing my eyes and putting my arms around his outline, the imagined shape of him. Hoping to hell this passes.

Least this way I don't have to get into it with him. School. All that. At least I don't have to face, I don't know, his disappointment. I can't stand the thought of his disappointment.

Coward, I know. Always.

I turn on the telly to a crackle of applause. Slick suit, jabbing his microphone at this woman in a bikini. Caption runs along the bottom: *TOO BIG FOR THE BEACH?*

What in the name of fuck. I lift the remote and flick: *Homes Under the Hammer...* some news thing with a panel... an old *Frasier...* Gordon Fucking Ramsay... three-hour remake of *King Kong...* cartoons... some reality thing in a salon... Christ on a bike.

Cycle path runs all the way from the Ocean Terminal to somewhere in the middle of the country. It's not a million miles to the New Town. I have it in my head I'm going to pop into the caff and say hello to Bartek, order him to make me one of his finest lattes, but by the time I get to Dean Bridge and climb the steps at Pizza Express my bottle's all the way gone. I loiter like a baddy on the corner across the road, watching the door, all the usual comings and goings. No sign of Bartek and I get to wondering if he's moved on too. People do come and go in that place.

For the sake of doing something I take out my phone and get a sugar rush from my messages. Brian wondering where I've been the past week. Carol checking in. *I'm fine*, I write back to both. *Let's get together soon. How are you?* Linger a wee minute for a reply but nothing doing.

Keep going, following the Water of Leith through the Dean Village and past the sign pointing upwards to the galleries, and that's when the rain comes on, of course. I find myself walking into it, shouting through my teeth as it gets worse. Opening my mouth, gargling with the wet stuff. Loony me. Stand under the bridge just before Roseburn for a moment letting my hands thaw. Nobody around so I open my mouth and yell a couple of times, just a single note, the sound coming up out of my guts. Me versus the downpour. The big man!

One foot then the other, on a mission to nowhere. Leaves plastered to the ground, everywhere underfoot. Mud streaking my shoes. I can keep moving, but whatever's behind is going to catch up eventually.

Old Jordan went away thinking I'm one thing, when I know I'm something else.

Better this way.

I mean, where to even begin?

So, Jordan, I was one of the ones that…

Me…

I was there when…

Me...
I put the boot in, not hard, but...
Okay, hard, but just the once or twice, like...

I can't think of that time without thinking about Hutton. I mean, I can't picture him, not properly. I don't even know what happened between us. One minute I was the wingman, always on hand to laugh at his jokes and shamble after. Then one day I walked into registration and heard my name followed by a silence, shuffling bodies, a few sniggers. I hadn't got the news. The whole group got up at the bell, and that was that. I was out. Now I was the one going around the edges of the field, kicking at cans, kicking up muck.

I know fine what happened.

It was the boys' changing room, just after PE. I was always last into the showers, slow as shite. I'd wait as long as possible, packing my stuff and slow stripping before grabbing my towel and running across the cold tiles.

Far as I knew I was the only body in the changing room but when I moved around the bank of lockers, there was Hutton, standing with his back to me. I just stood there, gawping at the long stretch of neck running from his hairline down into his clothes. As I watched he slid his T-shirt over his head and half turned to throw it into his bag.

My mind was just getting a sense of how skinny and knotty and kind of sweet he was when I realised he'd spun all the way round. I'd forgotten to lock my knees or square my shoulders. I was just standing there, dumbstruck.

Before I could even open my mouth he was hurtling across the room. I raised my hands. First punch grazed the side of my head, and then he'd got me by the throat. I kicked at his legs, swatting blindly. He brought his face up close, and I caught the sweet warmth of his breath. Heaved myself up and fought back until his grip slackened. I was raging. Jesus. I could be a bastard when I was in the mood. No idea what the hell I was doing, pushing and lashing out, real fucking fury behind the punches.

We broke apart. When I lifted my chin he flinched, and of course that made me feel amazing and sad at the same time. I searched for his eyes, but they'd disappeared behind a screen of hair. Another minute and we might have laughed, but instead he swung round to face his locker like nothing had happened.

There wasn't much more after that. School didn't so much end as peter out for me, and Hutton must have left the same year.

I saw him one more time after school ended, least I think I did. It was a Saturday afternoon. As I sat at the bus stop counting out my small change there was Hutton on the other side of the road. I waited a moment then I set off after him, followed him the short distance to the Dumbiedykes. He was fast. *Whoa. Whoa there.*

I watched him run up into block number two. Crouched behind a wall, wondering what to do, then went inside, but he was nowhere. I can still mind the stillness of the lobby, the weird clean smell, goosebumps as I watched the red-lit number 4 above the lift, wondering if it would move up or down. If he would come back down and catch me, or if I'd have the guts to go up there and find him, and even if I did, what would I say.

I scarpered. Course I did.

I've Googled him a couple of times, but nothing doing. Hutton Kern. Pretty sure there aren't many of them out there. But I'd love to know what happened to him. He wouldn't even be in my head now if it wasn't for Jordan, these last few days. Hutton. One of those faces from the old life that just fades and fades and fades. Wouldn't know him now.

*

I'm all the way to Murrayfield when my phone goes.

'Listen,' Frank says, or rather shouts. 'What you up to?'

I run a hand across my wet face, look across at the top of the rugby ground rising like a UFO. Wondering if I can resist. Wet fucking through. I swear to god my hair's become one with my forehead.

'Nothing,' I say sweetly into my phone. 'I'm not doing anything.'

Soon as I get to Willowbrae I get a sense something's up. Usually, Frank lets me in the way somebody with a cat might let puss in after a day's wandering. Today I've not even finished taking off my muddy shoes before he's got me wrapped up in a hug. I wait for him to soften. But no, this hug's strong and brisk, like one of my old boy's handshakes.

I follow him towards a rising smell of soup or stew, legs wrecked from my walk. By the time I reach the kitchen he's already got a towel for me and the red out the cupboard and poured, and I'm quickly woozy with it, wondering what the hell this is about. All throughout our lunch, while I'm steam drying across from him, he seems not himself. He's all pent up, babbling about things to do with his work, eyes on his plate.

I almost don't spot when he finally gets to his point. One minute he's saying something about interviewing some posh boy producer from Edinburgh's Hogmanay and the next he's telling me he's been invited to visit his brother William in New Zealand.

'I've never been down under,' he says, his voice going up on the last syllable, like something out of *Neighbours*, smiling to show me this is meant to be funny.

He's been saving all summer. Owes it to himself, he says: he hasn't had so much as a day off in he can't remember when.

I reach out and dump a load more wine in my glass. He puts down his cutlery all of a sudden.

'Maybe I should have said something to you earlier.'

I look down at my half-finished stew out the slow cooker. My first proper home-cooked hot meal in ages. There's Eve's pudding for afters.

'It's meant to be really beautiful over there this time of year,' he says.

'You're away soon, then?'

'Start of December.'

'You'll be gone for Christmas, then?'

He looks away, and I feel sorry and kind of stupid for pushing it. So I throw on a smile and get him to tell me about New Zealand and he sighs, like it's all a big pain in the backside really, this trip of a lifetime. He runs me through everything he wants to do with his visit, the shoulders slowly coming down, and after a while I find myself grinning along and meaning it, picturing him at the computer making plans, drawing up his itinerary.

'Sounds amazing.'

'The flight alone would kill you, Davie. Twenty-four hours.'

'They made *Lord of the Rings* there, right?'

'I couldn't get comfortable enough to sleep through that film...'

'Best film ever.'

'*David...*'

It's almost a reprimand. He closes his eyes for a moment, and when he opens them again, he says: 'Listen. I've met someone.'

'Uh-huh.' I suck at my wine.

'Ben. His name's Ben. We met online.' The next bit comes in a rush. 'He's a Geordie, you know, lives in Durham, but he's up and down here for family. He's a hack, too. Local paper, mostly. Some online.' He nods then, pressing his lips. 'He's just starting out, of course...'

'How old?'

'David.'

He straightens up, and his eyes are wide, and for a moment I feel like I don't know who he is. I'm looking at what he's wearing, too, this loose, flowery shirt with the sleeves rolled up at the bottom. He's brand new.

'That's... How long...?'

'A few months. Early days.'

'Still... New Zealand. New man.'

Who am I even kidding.

'I didn't know... I wasn't sure if I should tell you or not,' he says.

'Maybe I'll get to meet him sometime.'

'Well, you'll still be here when I get back.'

'Same as before.'

'Yes. Course.'

He's holding out a hand to me, relieved.

'It's been so difficult keeping all this from you,' he says, 'you've no idea.'

Apparently I'm supposed to take the hand. It's tough taking the hand while trying to drink up with the other.

'I remember when we met,' he says, holding my hand while looking down at the table. 'You and me. I was so happy. When I told people about you I just kept saying how gorgeous you were and how lucky I was. That's how I felt about you, Davie. I felt lucky.'

I can feel my hand twitching to get free.

'Now, it's all too much,' he's saying, 'all this coming and going. I think I was... I think we both need a clean break.'

I look down, making agreeing noises, and then, partly to stop him saying what he's saying, and partly because I need him to feel like he's not abandoning me or leaving me in the lurch or whatever, I blurt out: 'I've actually met someone too.'

'Oh.' He slowly pulls his hand away. 'But that's great. Right?'

'I mean, it's nothing really. An old... face from the past. No legs to it. Or arms, knees. Whatever. I mean, he's down south, I'm up here. London. It's nothing.'

'Well, that's a shame. Right?'

'I mean, it was nice, he was nice, but...' I lower my voice, like Jordan's in the corner, listening in on absolutely everything. 'Thing is, I think he might have a bit of a *drink problem*.'

'Ah. Okay.'

'I mean, he doesn't touch the stuff. Funny, right?'

'Teetotal, you mean?'

'Anyway, he's off back to London.'

'So that's that, then.'

'That's that.'

And we both shrug and swap these wee looks, pretending lightness. And almost right away I feel sore inside because I know I haven't done justice to Jordan, nowhere close, and Frank sees I'm upset and gets it all wrong by coming round the table to give us another back-breaking cuddle, and all I can think is, *get the fuck off me*.

We're both quiet for what feels like ages, sitting staring down at the table with our heads on the side, and I'm wishing I was gone. In fact, I'm sorry I even came, and god knows what he's thinking.

'You can stay here tonight if you like?' he says. 'We could catch up on some telly. We never finished watching *Baby Reindeer*.'

I'd be daft to say no. Staying, that's the easy option, the place so nice and familiar. And where the hell would I go now, anyway?

But I find myself standing and telling him no, it's fine, we'll make a date for soon. We'll have a wee shindig before he goes.

Get up from the table before I change my mind, feeling him behind me all the way to the door, thinking I could turn at any time and he'll be mine for the next few hours, him and Eve's pudding and this dry, cosy place, and Netflix until I'm stuffed like it's already Christmas, but I don't turn, I keep going, right through the door, and keep going.

Jordan

I let myself into Niall's empty hallway. Voices reach me from the other end of the flat, laughter rising and falling in an irregular rhythm. I wait a moment, but it's just the television, dialled a few notches louder than usual.

'Jordan? Jordy?'

The dark moves and my brother's face appears. He's wearing pyjamas and the outsized duffel coat with the Eskimo hood. He's carrying a coffee cup ever so daintily by the handle.

'Little bro.'

His free hand goes up to his head, trying to pick up the thread of something half remembered, but his smile's wrong like he's had his jaw numbed at the dentist. It's only when he moves towards me that I notice the smell coming from his cup.

'*Niall.*'

In that moment of disbelief, I make a grab. He pulls away, horrified, hugging the cup to his chest. He backs through the living room door, shaking his head. I throw out my arm again, my fingers finding the porcelain while Niall tightens his grip on the handle. The liquid jumps out and my wrists run brown.

I reach and take a hold of his arm, meaning to prise his fingers away with a single tug. Just then the handle comes off in his hand, sending me stumbling backwards. As the last of the cup bounces off the edge of the couch and dunts off the carpet Niall gives a sad grunt and throws the broken handle the length of the room. He falls square onto the couch and rolls onto his side, away from me.

'Where is it? Niall?'

He's made himself a foetus, his arms around his knees. I plunge in again, taking a hold of both wrists. We both let out a noise halfway between a giggle and a shout. We're kids again, toy fighting, exhilarated but aware it could all go too far.

As his arms lift apart the half bottle escapes and bumps to the floor.

We both scramble downwards but it's Niall who comes up first, his mouth ajar. He edges backwards on his knees, his arm flung back and wide. I go for his ankle and miss. He's on his feet now, sidestepping across the room. He slams the kitchen door so hard the frame trembles.

We face each other through the glass. Niall holds out a hand, palm-up like a stop sign, while he unscrews the cap with his teeth. About three inches left in the bottom. He spits the cap, lifts the bottle to his mouth, tips it up and sucks.

The first swallow brings such evident release to his body that I almost feel happy for him.

He wipes his chin.

Fine, you win.

I remember our father's friends used to compliment him on his high colour, as though he was just back from his holidays and was doing a grand job of holding on to his tan.

'Oh, that's just the drink,' he would say, and everyone would laugh, including me, even though I was complicit in the *real* black humour of the situation.

I'm angry with my brother for squandering his charm, the easy hand he was dealt. I want to grab him by the shoulders and shout: *What have you done to yourself!*

But my voice, when it comes, is clipped, take-charge.

'Come through here and have a seat, will you? Come on. I'll make us something to eat. Watch TV, if you like, remote's right there. What's this? *Holidays in the Sun?*'

'You're cooking?' His voice thick and slow. 'This I cannot wait to see.'

Still, he's obedient, edging around me in the doorway. I take up position in the middle of the kitchen and watch the steam rise from the kettle, the water heating for a meal I have no idea how to start. There's half a bag of pasta shells. The freezer's full up with slabs of meat. The fridge lets off a smell of ailing vegetables. A jar of capers. I salvage what I can then chop and cook with the radio tuned to one of those unbearable phone-ins.

My brother huffs around on the other side of the glass door, flicking between channels. I close my eyes and allow myself the picture of my one-bedroom flat, which is at least clean, and well-ordered. This time tomorrow I will be safely out of reach.

I sit Niall at the table and slide the plate under his nose. He cracks his neck, one side then the other. I used to find this hilarious when we were kids, the way it wound up our mother. He tests the pasta. 'Vegetarian?' He readjusts himself and pushes his fork in. He shovels up the plate of food like he hasn't eaten for a week.

'You used to let me watch you making the tea,' I say. 'Remember?'

'You were a quiet one. Wee ghost of the house. I always wanted to know what went on in that big brain of yours.'

'You used to indulge me. We made rock buns and tray bakes. That was all you.'

I watched him so closely back then. I tried to shrug myself into his skin, aping his stance. But it wasn't a comfortable fit for me.

'You showed me how to make a roux,' I say. 'I don't think I ate anything but macaroni cheese in my first year away from home.'

He faces forward, hunching over his empty plate.

'She's not coming, by the way. Rebecca.'

'But you... Claire...?'

'Claire's nothing to do with it.'

He turns away, sheltering his face in his hands. He breathes out a couple of times, and when he lifts his head, his eyes are damp.

'Claire was getting her ready and she... Rebecca got...' His shoulders jerk. 'She just doesn't want to see me.' A pause, and then he springs back in his seat with a force that makes me jump. 'So that's that, eh?'

I try to ignore the smell, the mix of sweet and sharp. I try to get out from under the image of our father, the remains of him oozing all over the kitchen table.

And I'm racking my brain, trying to think of something I can give him that's not Scottish Blend or the packet of half-coated biscuits I brought back with me from Mum's, when he starts coughing up a storm and I turn to see him extract himself with a lurching hop from the table.

The door bangs.

By the time I've cleared the plates and done the dishes, he's already been out and back with a couple of laden carrier bags, and my indignation has passed.

We sit together, watching television as though nothing has happened. Niall tugs on his beer. I sit at the end of the couch nearest the door. I keep my hand on the chair's arm so I can push myself up and exit stage right – all the way to London if I have to. Niall's staring at the screen, oblivious to the fact that I've got him caught in the corner of my eye.

A Western comes on.

'What's her name as an actress?' Niall says when John Wayne meets gutsy Laurie at the ranch.

'Vera Miles. She's the sister in *Psycho*.'

We both realise around the scene in the Comanche camp that we've seen the film before, so we fall to reminiscing. Remember when I tried to convince our parents to let me stay up and watch 9½ Weeks, claiming it was a romcom. Remember when our father came in from a night out and sang every verse of 'House of the Rising Sun' along with the record, surprising us all with his voice hitting the high notes. Remember the time we sat around the living room table with Niall's first serious girlfriend, Seonaid, a Morrissey fanatic.

'That's a very dramatic haircut you have there,' was all Mum could find to say.

We talk about the house at Drumbrae.

'Those fucking bunk beds,' Niall says. 'How did we manage to go all those years without killing each other?'

'You were all right – you had the bottom bunk. I kept hitting my head off the ceiling.'

'Mum spent her life fixing things.'

'And the creaking loft. You told me there was a poltergeist.'

'Did not.'

'Covers up to the chin. Terrified.'

We both return our attention to the television, and after a moment or two he stretches out, bunching his fists up under his chin.

'You want a blanket or something?'

'Nah.'

'Let me know if you do.'

'That was him,' he says, almost inaudibly.

'Sorry?'

'The poltergeist.'

I find the remote and silence the television.

'Peter,' he says. 'It was him in the loft, creeping around at night. He had a stash up there.'

Whenever he mentions our father, which isn't often, my instinct is to leap to his defence. For the moment, I don't say anything.

'Peter the poltergeist,' he smirks.

'He wasn't a bad man,' is all I say.

He doesn't respond, and that's fine. I'm not looking for anyone's validation.

'What time is it?' he says.

'Six. Up and at 'em.'

I start to rise.

'No, wait, will you?' His head drops, and when he lifts, I realise he's crying again.

'Niall.'

'Jordan. This thirst.'

I get up and sit on the arm of the sofa.

'You can stop again.'

'Jordan...'

'You can—'

'I'm trying. I'm *trying*.'

Ray Milland in *The Lost Weekend*. Like me, whether he realises it or not, he's a rent-a-quote for classic movies.

'Easier like this, eh?' He lets go a laugh, one of his abrupt, watery bursts. 'I should just let myself get on with it. Turn the rest of my life into pish.'

'All those months you managed it. Niall,' I say, and it's almost comic what comes out of my mouth next, the line I use with all my students, even the no-hopers. 'There is nothing stopping you but you.'

No response. For a moment I think he's tuned out, and who could blame him.

Then, as if he can no longer restrain himself, his voice comes, quick and breathless.

'Listen, Jordy, I need to tell you...'

He scrabbles up, a sense of urgency to his movements.

'Start of the summer there, not that long after me and Claire... Anyway, I was coming out of work, and it was hot, one of the really hot days we got at the end of May there. Everybody looked fuckin... boiled! Pouring onto St Andrew Square, knocking into each other, wanting to get home or to the gardens for a stretch out on the grass, catch the rays.

'And I knew where I was going. Straight to Oddbins like a fucking laser beam. I'd have a seat in Victoria Park with the taps-aff brigade. I'd be lively by five, blazing by eight.'

I hear him take another heavy breath.

'And I'm just heading along the square when I hear my name, and it's this woman from the office. Lesley Culvert, her name is, and she's... nice, you know. My age. Two boys at Broughton. She heads up the team next to mine, quality checking the new business. We'd been in a meeting last thing, Lesley and me and all the big cheeses. I'd barely said a word the whole time we were in there, and when I picked up my notepad at close of play all I'd written was *ODDBINS* at the top of the page. Can you believe it?'

He laughs then, with real merriment, as though he's recounting something that happened to someone else.

'So, there I am, and Lesley's saying my name, and I'm thinking please, not now. And she's all embarrassed, this Lesley, out of breath from racing down the road. Says she tried to catch me when I left, but I was on a mission... And we're standing there, bad-mouthing the boss, going back over this or that shit memo from on high, and Lesley's making some comment about how she's always scared to catch my eye in meetings for fear we'll crack up, it's happened before, and next thing, she's putting a hand on my arm and telling me she'd heard about me and Claire and she hopes I don't mind, she doesn't want to poke her nose in, but she got divorced a couple of years back, and she knows how tough it can be and if I ever want to talk, well, she's been told she's a good listener.'

He breaks off, and in that moment, I become aware of my knee, sharpened to a perfect point of pain. I try to readjust without breaking his flow.

'Thing is, she's something else. Lesley. No two ways. She's the dynamo of the floor. But, as she's saying all this, and I'm looking down into her smiling face, I start getting the sweats. My hands, my upper lip, my back – feels like I'm *leaking*. I start hopping from foot to foot. All I can think about is Oddbins and a soft landing in Victoria Park. And, and…'

I can feel him shifting, getting agitated.

'Aye, so I'm leaning away from her, wondering if she'll say cheerio and let me get on my way, and that's when I see him, just up the road a few yards. A suit, with his jacket hanging from his fingers and his tie like a noose.

'He's watching me from just up the street. He looks white as a sheet and just a right fucking state. Horrible. And he's looking right at me.'

I feel him sit up, leaning towards me.

'I mean, it sounds a joke. There's Lesley, still rattling away at my side, and all I can think is, Christ, it's him.'

'I'm not with you.'

'Peter.'

'Niall…'

'I know. But the thought settled itself in my head – it got into my head. And, well, you can just imagine. That feeling of just… complete… disconnect. I'm standing there, running all over with sweat and looking right across the street at my long-deceased father. And it's muggy as hell, and there's all these… *people*. And Lesley's voice going beside me. All I can do is shut my eyes and try to stay standing.'

'Niall…'

He draws himself up where he's sitting, and as I turn to him, he coughs out another great laugh.

'Sorry, your face.'

'What?'

More hoarse laughter, unrestrained.

'Look like you've seen a ghost.'

'Niall, I swear,' I say, even though I never swear if I can help it. Our mother was not a fan of *language*.

In his tiny kitchen I make myself a cup of tea, banging and rattling to cover the snap of the ring pull on his latest can. Part of me doesn't want to go back to the sofa, but I can't help it. I have to pull on the cord of his story and find out what happened next.

According to Niall, it must have taken a split second, less, for him to realise that what he was actually seeing was his own reflection in a funny-shaped mirror in the window of Harvey Nicks. But time had slowed, and as that split second stretched itself out, there was our father, it was him, staring at Niall from inside the magic mirror.

And, Lesley, poor Lesley, was in full flow, but he turned away, cut her off, not even a goodbye, just staggered to the side and threw himself into the stream of bodies flowing down Multrees Walk.

'Oddbins,' Niall says, 'I kept trying to keep Oddbins in my mind like a beacon, but something still wasn't right. I couldn't... I just couldn't get that fucking picture out of my head. Peter. I slowed to a plod at the pedestrian crossing on Queen Street. Came to a complete standstill in the island in the middle of the road. All I could do was stare down at my shoes. I found the railing and leaned against it. Heart *hammering*. Thought that was me. The crossing beeped god knows how many times, and my wee island kept suddenly filling with people. I clung on to that railing for dear life.'

As quietly as I can, I slide to the floor, the pain in my knee ebbing. I feel for my cup and stare stubbornly ahead, resistant, still half certain Niall's story will turn out to be some convoluted joke.

'So, I started counting,' he says. 'Just breathing and counting, turning and stepping, heading back to the side of the road I'd come from. Waited until I could catch a full breath then went all the way back round St Andrew Square. I had it in my head that I'd find Lesley and apologise, but she was long gone, and so off I walked around until I found a taxi to take me back to the flat. Dropped my coat on the floor in the hall and went straight to bed. Covers over the head. Haven't cried like that since I was a kid.'

I hear him catch his breath.

'In the morning it was like something had flipped in my brain. I started with the sheets on my bed. Pulled the hoover out and flew around like I was on something. The flat was full of empties. Anything that wasn't empty went down the sink. I bagged up all the rubbish and put it out to the bucket. Stour everywhere. I threw open the windows and then I just fuckin *cleaned*. And when I'd finished and I was standing there in my jockies, with the spray bottle in one hand and the cloth in the other, I looked around and didn't recognise the place.

'And I was thirsty. Man was I ever *thirsty*.'

His turn to look at me now. I can feel him, watching for my reaction.

'There was nothing to take me out of myself here. I'd moved in with a wee suitcase and a bag of messages. I had to take myself out for a drive so I wouldn't do anything daft. Mile after mile. Ended up in the Borders of all places – Tweedbank! Eating a fish supper on a bench at the side of a duck pond. Sunset was really fucking… gorgeous. I tried to get hold of Claire before I set off for home, but she was out, or she wasn't answering. Bottled leaving her a message. *I'm doing great* was what I wanted to say to her. *Think I'm on the up.* Thank god she wasn't answering her phone…

'And all the way home I couldn't stop thinking about that burn on the back of your tongue, the first cold taste. The way it starts to feel sore when you're on your seventh or eighth. Or thirtieth. The way it soaks and coats, until you're numb all the way to your ends.

'And all I could think was, I can't stop. I have to stop.'

'You did stop, Niall,' I say. 'You stopped.'

After a moment, he eases himself downwards, so we're both on the floor, with our backs against the sofa, staring at the window, the trees outside shadow-patterned against the night sky.

'Last time I went over to the house, Rebecca was on her beanbag looking at one of her programmes,' he says. 'Didn't even look up or say hello. Claire coaxed her away from the telly, and she stood in front of us with her eyes searching the floor, hands twitching at her side. Then she raised her head, which I took as a sign to put out my arms for a cuddle, and I had my mouth ready to say something when she took a breath and started reeling off everything she'd learned at the school that day. It was all solar system and planets and the Earth's distance from the sun. All in a big rush. And she kept glancing around me, trying to find Claire...'

'Niall—'

'No, listen—'

'You're not him. You're not Peter.'

He just snorts.

'You know, it wasn't so much the shock of seeing him looking back at me from my own fucking reflection that stayed with me while I drove hard to the Borders that day. It was the thought of poor Lesley. That nice Lesley left babbling to herself in the middle of the street. That left me... guilty as hell.'

I gulp my tea. He's already said a lot, and I'm still trying to take it in.

'I went back to work on the Monday,' he says. 'Told her I was sorry as soon as I saw her and of course she just laughed, saying we all have our off days. Oh, come here, she says, and she gives me this massive cuddle and tells me the offer stands: I can come to her any time I want to talk. I get it, she says.

'And I managed a smile, but I just couldn't look her in the eye. She's just so forgiving, and that's... that's the worst.'

*

Sometime later, I hear the papery rustling, the fag sparking to life.

'I don't get it,' he says on the inhale. 'I mean, how come you never...?'

I wish I had an answer for him. You'd think I'd have worked something out by now. I've been fielding the question all my adult life. Parties, gatherings, meals out: *You don't drink? Is there something the matter with you?*

There's always a moment, entering a room full of that acerbic smell, when my stomach gives a quiet lurch. And then, just as quickly, it recedes, becoming just another part of the evening. And I can live with it, the smell, in the air and out of glasses. Even the taste of it, fiery or faint, on another person's tongue can bring back associations, surprisingly pleasant memories.

But I don't have the taste, I never have, and it won't help Niall to hear that I don't know why. Sure, it wasn't fun seeing my father useless with drink every day for years. But Niall and I both learned at our father's knee. How we ended up drawing such different lessons, well, there's the mystery of it.

He makes a sound, quite soft, and smoke balloons upwards.

'We tried to keep things from you, Jordan,' he says.

I know.

'The worst of it.'

'Let's not talk about this.'

'Sure, he loved us, he must have *loved* us, Jordy, but it got so he couldn't *see* us anymore. Mum used to send me out looking for him when he didn't come home after the pub was shut. You didn't know that did you?'

I was there, remember?

'This once, I found him spark out under the swings in the park. Bunch of wee neds standing around flicking snot at him. Sent them scattering. Then I was up the town after school one day and I had to step over him and a whole bunch of his pals to get up a flight of steps from Holyrood to the Pleasance. Too out of it to notice me.'

Whoosh, another cloud at the height of my head.

'Another night, I had to help him out of the bushes at the edge of the path that ran alongside the railway. He'd pulled his coat around him – the plan was to spend the night there, in all the muck and mud, the idiot. Middle of January, he might have frozen to death, and he was the one giving out at *me* for waking him.'

His dander's up. I'm not required for this rant. I want to tell him out loud that I know. I saw it all and more, and I've heard these stories before.

This is why I stay away.

I asked our mother once if she missed Dad, and this was her reply, eloquent as ever.

'If I'm happy enough, on form, I let myself think of the man who used to phone me up at work for his lunchtime catch-up, not saying much, just listening and making all the right noises while I ran down my list of grievances. He did this every day for years. I think of that Peter, and I can feel the weight...'

She put a hand to her chest, pressing the tips of her fingers.

'Maybe if I'm up too early after a poor night's sleep, I find myself picturing him as he was later on – the way he would panic and get animated if the telly changer was on the other side of the room. I try to avoid that Peter. I have to get up and move around, move away from him, and sometimes, god help me, I feel so relieved that he can't come after me, that I've got this piece of my life all to myself.'

She got up then, and started on whatever or whoever it was she had to manage next.

*

'I'm not him, Jordy,' Niall says, and neither of us knows if it's a statement or a question.

He flicks his butt away, and I take note of where it lands so I can clear up later.

He pulls himself back up onto the couch. I hear him shrugging himself into a comfy position.

'Niall, are you sure you don't want a blanket?'
'Nah.'
'Let me know if you do.'
'What time is it?'
'Back of nine.'
'Ten o'clock, give's a nudge,' he says. 'I have to phone home.'
'Yep.'
'Don't let me forget.'
'I won't forget.'

Davie

All the way to the Regent. Mister Fucking Predictable.

I order my vodka, positioning myself so I can see the room. I like it when there's a decent crowd in, all the folk who've forgotten or don't care it's a school night. Guns N' Roses on the jukebox. Suppose you can't have everything.

A wavy-haired skinny guy's sitting at a table on the other side of the bar. As he leans to the side he squints in my direction, and I realise I know him. Rab. Yet another friend of Frank's. The two of them were in the same year at the school: they played in bands together when they were younger. Frank sang a bit and Rab played the bass. People said Frank brought him out of himself, but that's bullshit. Frank brought Rab to pubs. It was the drink that brought Rab out of himself. Lush Rab, Frank calls him and not because he's fit. I've rarely seen him when he wasn't paggered.

Now he's rising from his perch and moving towards me, getting bigger as he sidles between the tables. As he gets close he's still smiling, though now he's swithering, the doubt pulling at his face.

'Yeah, it's me, Rab. Davie.'

A real lived-in face. Bags under the eyes, the whole caboodle. We find a table, and he plops down opposite. He takes a drink then sighs through his teeth.

'Yeah,' he says, 'just the ticket. You on your own?' A wee drop at the end of each phrase. He's well on.

'How's tricks, Rab?'

'Oh terrible, awful. Unbearable. Don't ask.'

He fixes me with a look that says: *ask*. I start him off with a nod and as he chugs away I sit back and drink, throwing in the odd question. That's the thing about Rab, he's always got a plan. The latest thing is that he wants to own his own guesthouse; be his own boss. If something came up in Scotland he'd be happy, but he'd rather set up abroad: Mallorca, Ibiza, Greece, the Canaries.

'Sounds interesting,' I say, knowing it'll never happen.

We tan the beers and Rab becomes a Ready Brek blur in my eyes. Bell clangs for last orders.

'Wait. How did that happen?'

'I've got more drink back at mine,' says Rab, quiet in case the whole pub hears and wants in.

So, we're soon outside again, weaving down towards Rab's in Abbeyhill. A voice in my ear: *You're really going to do the deed with Lush Rab?* And, I'm thinking, no, I'd have to be nuts. *For real?* says the voice. I shake myself, half at the cold and half to get rid of the wee voice, and follow him down a cracked path with weeds exploding out the gaps, through a door and up a few steps into a close stair.

By the time we get to his hallway the voice has gone completely and all I want out of life is to see Rab out his trousers. I make straight for the bedroom, pitching sideways, dunting off the walls, but Rab has other ideas: he shouts me into the kitchen, goes straight to the freezer and gets out the Grey Goose.

'Heating's on the blink.'

We sit in his cold kitchen in our jackets, passing the Goose back and forth. Mostly in silence, though he gets up to fiddle with his radio, sliding through Christmas tunes and classical stuff until he lands on 6 Music with a happy shout.

He dumps himself back down and rattles off a few questions. How's the work been? How's the flat?

'All good.'

He keeps saying sorry. Sorry, sorry, sorry, ashamed for not being in touch. He's not forgotten about me, he says, it's just that sometimes he forgets we're not together anymore, me and Frank. He hopes we can still be pals. Sure, whatever. His cold kitchen's making me sad. I reach for his lapels and get a clumsy vodka kiss for my pains. He slips to the side, and I feel his head heavy on my shoulder. We get up, tipping against each other, the one supporting the other. In the kitchen doorway he makes a feeble effort to unbuckle my breeks and then there's an unreal swirl of lobby and bedroom, Rab's thin face rotating against the Paisley pattern of his bedclothes, and finally there's just Rab, lying on his back half on and half off the bed, with his mouth open and the neck of the Grey Goose in his fist.

'Wake the fuck up!'

He mutters and rolls on his side. I'm kind of raging. I stand there a moment then pull at the covers, tuck him in gently. One last thing. I prise the bottle out of his grip and hit the stairs, swigging.

Soon as I'm outside I feel mortal with the drink. I have to stop and hold myself against the gate. Wind nudges as I step off the kerb and I tumble to my knees. There goes my vodka, all over the road. *Fuck*. Hoist myself back up, and I find that I'm laughing, ending myself actually. It's all kinds of funny.

Oh Frank, if you could see me now.

As I clip down the road bits of him glimmer before my eyes: the long, stiff eyelashes, the hollow bit at the base of his throat, that slight softness at his belly, the fan of soft hair at the top of his backside.

Frank.

Need to get home. Netflix. *Baby Reindeer*. I fantasise putting my arms around him, feeling him wrap me close. I lean into the cold air, picturing him opening the door to me at the other end, but when I get down to Jock's Lodge people get between us in the street. I push back, elbows out. I feel brave, the kind of brave you feel when there's someone waiting for you at the other end.

Heads turning. One guy looks like he wants to take a swing. Oh, but I'm queasy. I have to stop by a bin and take a few breaths to stop myself boaking.

Keep going. I could walk this route blindfold. Shield my eyes against the outside light and climb up to the door, wishing I'd brought something, flowers or some more meaningful gift, a token of my homecoming.

Knock, knock. Ring, ring.

'Frank?'

Miraculously, I've still got my keys. Fumble them into the lock and push with my shoulder.

'Frank?'

Desperate for a pish. The bathroom door's a sheet of mist at the end of the landing. I batter it open, making a grab for the light, and stand there doing my business while shouting his name, *Frank, Frank, Frank*, like a wee yappy dog.

Kitchen on the left, our room on the right, the door still wide to the world. My every move makes the place swirl. Whole house is a mystery.

Frank?

I go back into the bathroom. Rain against the skylight. I sit down on the edge of bath, peering upwards, like he might be there, clinging to the ceiling like Spidey.

And then it's like my whole self goes up a gear. Where the fuck? I go from room to room, pushing open the doors, pulling open the cupboards. *Where are you?* I pull down the ladder from the ceiling and climb. Crawl like a commando through the loft, punching aside Christmas decs, piles of old presents, old boxes of shit.

I sink down onto the floor in the darkness and sit among the chaos for ages. Or maybe just for a few minutes. I've lost track of the time.

Frank?

Head's a riot. Big-top circus. It's almost funny. Everything spinning, whirling, even when I close my eyes. 'Frank?' I say, trying out my voice, but I'm near hoarse: 'Frank?' Hands in my pocket to stop them getting froze. Can't stay here, bunched up in the dark. Mad. Madwoman in the attic. Need to get out of this attic. One, two, three, heave-ho…

Back in the bedroom, I get on the empty mattress. Curl up and try to imagine there's someone there beside me. Frank. Jordan. Warm to the touch. And I'm thinking I don't know what I'd rather have. The feel of him, there on the bed, the weird comfort of him. Or knowing, really knowing with no more pissing about, that this part of the story's over.

Sometimes I dream we're still together, me and Frank. So vivid it feels real. I wake from these dreams, my body jolted by some weight at the other end of the bed. I lie there, waiting, but even half asleep I know I'm alone.

There's a word I hate.

Alone.

I just don't know how to be alone.

Jordan

I sleep in snatches, hunched on the couch, aware that Niall's up and moving around well before the light. He's always had the ability to drag his remains out of bed no matter how much he'd put away the night before. Our father was the same. Lazy bedding was considered a waste of good drinking time.

'That's me away, then.'

He's standing at the foot of the couch, rolling one of his home-made cigarettes. Hair shined to the squeak. There's something of the waxwork about him.

'You're going into work?'

'Nothing else for it.' He chucks the finished roll-up from one palm to the other, gradually opening the gap between his hands. 'What time's your train?'

'Eleven-thirty. I'm scuzzy, I need a shower. Give me a minute and I'll walk out with you.'

I pull back the cover and there's the sleeve of the jumper I wore all day yesterday. My mouth feels dry. In all the drama of last night I forgot to brush my teeth.

Niall brings the rolly to rest in his right hand, and for a moment he stays there, the uncertainty of yesterday nearly but not quite gone from his face.

'Thought I might go out to Queensferry after work. Claire's idea.' The frown deepens. 'Apparently I texted her last night.'

'You did...?'

'Something about... oh, everything's great, everything's coming up roses.'

He moves to stand by the window and pulls the curtain back, pretending to look but really half hiding.

'Claire thinks it might be better if Rebecca sees me out at the house,' he says. 'We can have a bite and then maybe a go on the swings. She says we need to be patient, give her time. Don't push it, she says. She's right.'

He leans back, and I notice a trace of a smile, in spite of himself: the image of Claire or Rebecca, or the both of them, perking him up for a moment.

He moves towards the window again, the curtain concealing him.

'I don't want to be this guy she hides from whenever I come into the room, you know? I want her to see me and smile. I want to be able to scoop her up when I come in the door. No need to ask permission. But Claire's right, I have to be careful.'

He steps back, and as he straightens up and inhales I sense him collecting up everything he spilled out into the room last night and returning it to its rightful place, locking it and putting the key on a high shelf. Now he's Roy Scheider in *All That Jazz*. Showtime!

He turns to me then with his professional smile. How did I sleep? he asks. Am I all set for the off? Have I said my goodbyes to Mum? All the while he keeps glancing downwards at his tightening cigarette, barely nodding at my replies. I'm not sure which version of my brother is more infuriating: this automaton or Mister Messy.

Some part of me wants to try reaching for him. Instead, I lean back on the couch and rearrange the covers around me. I'm wrapped up like I've got the flu.

He lifts his ciggy. Then, finding no lighter or matches to hand, he drops it in his top pocket. My suited brother: I try to imagine what his colleagues make of him. Do they see a middle manager straight from central casting with the usual tired eyes? Do they notice the length of his eyelashes, that dimpled smile? I remember him when he was all ligaments and cartilage. He used to take the stairs of our apartment block three at a time.

'Niall.'

He stops by the door.

'It's all going to work out – with Rebecca. I really believe that.'

'Is that so?'

I hear the weariness in his voice. But this is overlaid by something else, a certain reproach: the tone he'd use when we were kids and I was trying to talk to him about something outwith my experience, like French kissing or a programme that was on past my bedtime. *What would you know?*

It's bright out, one of those rare sunglasses-and-scarf days: the kind that fools you into thinking the winter won't be as much of a drag as you'd feared. Niall offers to carry my bag and I knee-jerk refuse, but after a couple of hundred yards it's hitting off my legs in an obnoxious way, so he flicks his fag and silently puts out his hand for it. He doesn't seem in much of a hurry to get to the office, almost as though he used up all his reserves of energy getting dressed.

It's Monday morning, but it's Sunday-quiet on the Walk with the remnants of the weekend still blowing around the pavement. I steer him and the bag he's effortlessly carrying towards the café I ate in with David, the one I half remembered from childhood. With one hand deep in his pocket, he lifts my holdall ahead of me up the steps, apparently unfazed by this pitstop. The place is empty save for a cluster of student types from the hostel up the road, raincoats over the backs of their chairs. One white-haired woman sits alone by the window, her head quivering in excitement at every small shift or sound.

Is this where we came as a family all those years ago? Even the shape of the space seems different. Our table was somewhere near the back, I seem to remember. We could watch the staff coming and going through the swing doors with plates up their arms.

'Niall, do you remember this place?'

'Used to be a diner,' he says. 'We came here once or twice.'

'Wasn't it lovely,' I say.

He looks across. He's wearing our mother's expression, mystified, but there's a shy smile to go along with it.

Niall goes up to get our coffee and breakfast. The vegetarian option for me, which of course he has to question more than once.

I glance at the table by the window. Some involuntary tic makes me hunt out my phone and the number I haven't yet deleted. I wonder about taking a picture of the empty table and sending it to David. *Wish you were here.* I wrinkle my nose at the naffness of this idea, but I continue to lurk behind my phone, wondering how to reach out in a dignified way.

Back in Element for one last hurrah, if you're around?

Well, what's the worst that could happen?

Jordan, I think there has been a...

I press send then turn innocently towards the window.

As Niall returns I'm thinking how nice it is to be here with him. Niall, in his disguise as an office worker, all shining hair and acumen, unable to stop himself wrinkling his nose in disgust at the oboe opener of 'A Winter's Tale' by David Essex.

The next contact we have will be a WhatsApp message about how my train journey went. Maybe if I'm lucky a call at Christmas. Then little or nothing for a while.

At least he's there in my phone, Niall, one thumb-push away. I don't want him becoming someone whose face I can barely conjure without a photograph.

One morning, a few months before I left school, my father lifted his head all the way from his chest and noticed I had fuzz on the end of my chin.

'What age are you now, then?'

When I told him I was seventeen the news brought sudden colour to his face.

'Well, I'll need to be taking you out for a pint.'

We arranged to meet up outside the Assembly Rooms on George Street after I'd finished school for the day. I was amazed to find him there, standing next to the arched entrance with his back to me, one hand outstretched as though testing the strength of the wall. He'd worn a rucksack over his sweater and the hump of his back made him look like a tourist.

I began to wonder what I would say to him, how I would introduce myself. I wasn't used to meeting up with him in this way. He never ventured out in those days. It was almost a miracle to find him in the arranged spot. But then he turned and saw me ('Jordan!'); and the sudden laugh, the wide-eyed look made something turn light inside me.

He lumbered across the road, signalling with a roll of his shoulders for me to follow. My father took his time at every set of lights, snapping his eyes left and right, gathering the nerve to cross. It took the longest time to find a pub that would admit me in my school uniform. He pulled me through the crowded bar to a wooden table not much bigger than a footstool, letting his rucksack fall down his arms.

I think he was wearing a hoodie with a chewed-up drawstring. It might have been Niall's, or it might have been mine, or I might have made it up. How old his face looked above that worn teenage garment, and how confused, his head flicking in the direction of every raised voice.

'Know what? It's early but I might just have a pint,' my father said, as though the occasion demanded a treat. 'What about you? What do you drink?'

Jordan. My name is Jordan.

When I told him I wanted a Coke he nodded, seemingly having forgotten the whole rite of passage thing this was meant to be, the pint glass being passed down from one generation to the next. In his eyes I was still twelve years old, though I was by now taller than him. I'm not even sure he saw me at all. I wasn't Jordan so much as a breathing human who was available to sit in the pub and keep him company.

There was a moment of drama because he didn't have enough cash to pay for two drinks. I went into the zip pocket of my bag and pulled out the tenner I carried for emergencies.

He stared for a moment. 'Oh aye. Oh yes.' He slid the note off the table. When he heaved himself back up again the effort, or maybe the relief, had caused his face to flush in its alarming way. The money wasn't mentioned again.

While he clung to the bar I had a look in his rucksack. There was nothing inside except for a number seven bus timetable and a bit of paper with his name, address and phone number written on it in my mother's handwriting.

I could have left him to the money and drinks. He wouldn't have minded me not being there. Someone else from the pub would help him to the bus stop. But I felt determined to see out our date in the busy bar with its oddly consoling smell.

When he came back to the table I found I couldn't tear my eyes away from his face as he drank. It was like one of Hitchcock's expressive close-ups. His eyes were bright, but not with health.

My father lifted his head from his pint, frowning, seemingly surprised to find me still there. His gaze settled on one of the striped lines of my school tie. His hands groped around his cold glass until he found the right words.

'Aye, so how's the school treating you?'

My chest warmed. At last, I rushed him through my progress in history and chemistry while he drank with his lips clamped to the rim of the glass.

Blurred Faces

And even as I was saying all my lines I could feel him fading, losing interest in my small achievements as the beer began to work its magic and the next pint called from the bar. Smoke billowing from a neighbouring table stung my eyes. I kept talking, my voice stretching across the table in an effort to keep my father in place. I suddenly realised that I was shouting, and that people were turning from the bar, turning and leaning away, wondering why the camp schoolboy was yelling at this shrunken old man.

But I remember the times when I felt my father's love, the value of it. At night he'd always told me stories he made up himself, with heroes whose first name was the same as mine. Some evenings, as we ate, I would catch him looking at me sideways, smiling.

He ribbed Niall about his many girlfriends, but he would gently shut down anyone else's attempt to draw me out on my non-existent love life.

'Jordy's not one for the girls,' he'd say, placing a hand on my shoulder, and I was, for a moment, scared, because I realised he knew, even though I thought I had hidden it well, and I knew he would keep my secret.

And later on, I'd look at our father from time to time, wondering if the person he'd been – the electrician and storyteller and instructor – was still in there, somewhere.

Niall's attention is on the door, which is being negotiated by a youngish woman with a three-tier buggy. He springs up and holds it open, and the woman lets loose a stream of gratitude and a shy smile, prompting Niall to counter with one of his own. I enjoy the scene, inwardly cheering as he takes both ends of the buggy to carry it down the steps.

I use the moment to find my phone and scroll to my mother's number. The ringtone gives way to voicemail. It's funny, the time it takes for her voice to come on the line. She has softened her accent, rounding the vowels the way she thinks people are meant to talk when they're on the telephone.

Whenever my friends elsewhere asked about where I came from I found I could easily shift the conversation away. It wasn't hard. I had other things to answer for and explain in those days. Was I gay? Bi? No judgement, they just wanted a straight answer. To most of them, Scotland meant *Braveheart*, and if they were really engaged, certain bands, certain books, the new parliament. I was only interesting by virtue of having insight into one or two things the people around me didn't know about.

I learned to be selective in what I shared. I learned to flatten my accent, avoid words my friends wouldn't understand. I kept my father from them.

When I did go home from university, which wasn't often, I saw Dad only when he was lucid, sitting up. I was able to look past his tiny frame, and into his unguarded eyes.

'How are things with you, then?'

Jordan. My name is Jordan.

According to Mum, he was proud that I'd gone away to study. Any mention of me, she said, made him sit forward, all ears.

I arrived at the hospital in time to see him. At least, a version of him. He lay with his head sunk into the pillows, eyes staring up at the ceiling. His arms were pinned to his sides on top of the covers, his wrists manacled to the bed by two sets of hands. One of these belonged to a woman, my mother. The other set of hands, darker, heavier, belonged to a man sitting with his back to me. My brother. Whenever Mum glanced across the bed for reassurance, he responded by nodding or shaking his head and tightening his grip on Dad's wrist. They seemed together.

Blurred Faces

I moved as close as I could without drawing attention to myself. When had I last seen my father? Months earlier. When did we last have a conversation of more than half a dozen words? I stood for a moment, willing him to look at me.

But he just carried on staring at the ceiling, mouth softly open.

On the day of the funeral, Niall and I sat up late together. After the usual stories had been dragged out and laughed at hard, my brother went back to the morning of our father's final collapse. Niall had got the phone call from Mum while he was getting ready to leave the house. Dad had fallen out of bed, and she was having trouble moving him. As he told me what had happened, Niall kept moving around in his chair, his face tight at the memory of racing to the flat and arriving to find Dad fading in Mum's arms.

He was looking at me as though he expected some kind of response. I couldn't tell Niall I was sorry I had missed out on the experience because it wasn't what I felt. I was practised at moving on, forgetting.

'I really do have to get to work,' says Niall.

'If I'm not careful I'll miss my train.'

But the sun is out now and brightening the window of the café. We both embrace it, something funny in the sunlamp warmth to the strains of the Waitresses' 'Christmas Wrapping'.

'Too early,' he says. 'Way too early to be jolly.'

'I think this might be my favourite Christmas song of all time.'

'Mine too,' he says.

I picture Niall's face as he was at the window this morning, unable to speak without the cover of the curtain. I think about my mother: how amiable she was when she said goodbye the other day. Both of them mine, and both so nearby.

'I'll get this,' says Niall, taking out his card.

We stand at the counter while the guy rings through the order, and a great sad blast comes in through the door and throws its weight against me. The café's filling. I hear my mother telling me I'm the best-travelled person she knows, smiling with vicarious pleasure. Things happen at home, and I stay outside of it all, rootless and freewheeling. The well-travelled son. My family expect nothing of me now. We dance around each other in a way that makes me want to scream.

As Niall heads for the gents, the door to the café opens again, and I turn, shading my eyes. The new entrant's head is bent towards the ground, his gait dragging his shoulders forward. He jerks his eyes up, and there he is, with absolute clarity.

I'd never really noticed before how much he walks with his head down, like he's trying his very hardest to avoid the rest of humanity.

I can do no more than wave, a precious flutter.

'Thought that was you away,' he says.

'You came. How are you doing?'

'See it all, you know...'

He breaks off, abashed, and I start wondering how to respond or whether I can touch him, and there's an odd moment when my brother joins us, and we stand all three together. I make the introductions, and there's a mention of school, which always sets off a frisson in me, but to which Niall only gives a disinterested nod.

My brother and I say our goodbyes while David's at the counter. I receive a handshake and a mock punch to the chin and a *here's looking at you, kid*.

As he goes towards the door, he turns and gives a kind of salute, and maybe I imagine it, but it seems his smile wavers. Then he squares his shoulders, becoming his functioning self.

A moment earlier I might have been tempted to go after him, but now it doesn't feel so hard to let him walk away. I hesitate there at the door, watching him stretch himself out as he makes his way uphill. Niall. Maybe I've made a mistake, pinning my hopes on some imagined look or feeling, but whatever the case, I'm not ready to give up on him yet.

David is not so much leaning as lying over the counter, waiting for his order. He's innocent with fatigue, his hair standing out at a jaunty angle.

'Don't even tell me I look like shite,' he says. He nods towards my watch. 'You set? Better get a move on.'

He won't look me in the eye. Every movement seems an effort for him. I see his face change; we both look down, and there it is, my hand on his hand, on the counter.

'You okay?' he says.

'There's nothing – it's nothing. I didn't know if you'd come, and now. I've missed my train. Or it's missed me. And I'm still here. Like the song. You don't know it. No. Well, it's nice out, and I fancy a walk. Come on. Do you fancy a walk?'

Davie

Rare bright day. Light brings the top of the city up clear. I wrap myself up in my jacket and lift my head to warm my face and for a minute I'm all kinds of happy.

We start off taking it in turns lugging his bag, but it gets old quickly, so we end up sticking it in left luggage at Waverley then head out the back of the station, away from the crush. Reels of place names behind us: *Haymarket, South Gyle, Dalmeny, Inverkeithing, Dalgety Bay, Aberdour...*

On the way towards Holyrood, we pass under the rail bridge and Jordan double-takes at the crater where they're building the new hotel complex.

'Used to be a bus garage.'

We both say it at the same time.

I remember a club night too, back when they still had dancing in the town, and a Saturday market that did handmade jewellery and tie-dyed clothes and all kinds of nice crap.

We've reached the corner where Calton Road meets the Mile, and you can hear the bagpipes out of the gift shop beside Holyrood Palace. Tartany version of 'Smoke on the Water'. There are bunches of tourists, all with massive umbrellas under their arms, trudging downwards.

'Let's go on up the Crags,' says Jordan, one hand on my sleeve, the other pointing up at the wedges of rock. He stops a wee minute and checks his knee, then shrugs and says, 'Yeah, I think I want to go up,' and I'm more than happy to keep going, because if I stop moving I think that might be me for the rest of the day.

Path goes up at a steeper angle than I remember. My pins keep giving up the ghost because I've got on these daft trainers and Jordan has to keep pulling me up, which makes him wince, so I get worried about his knee. By the time we get up on the flat I've almost no breath. Both of us panting. Sky seems bigger than ever: just a few white streaks against the blue, and all the noise left behind.

He's smiling in that hundred per cent way he has. I try to respond in kind, even though my hands are shaking, my breath hard in my lungs, and not just for the climb and the cold. I've all of a sudden got the image of Jordan's brother, Niall, right at the front of my brain. The look he gave me in the café. No words, just a quick jab of the eyes. Like he could see my thoughts. I tried to smile. He didn't smile back, and I didn't say another word, just eyes on the floor. Praying Jordan wouldn't leave the two of us alone together for fear of small talk or something worse.

Who knows what he remembers about me. I don't know and it can't be helped.

We crouch in the cold and try our damnedest to sit and admire the city, the whole of Auld Reekie laid out in a circle below us: the old town at the centre, all the buildings stacked on top of each other, all the way up to the castle on its perch.

Jordan bounces up once or twice to take pictures. He fiddles with his phone, stringing them all together to make a landscape.

Below us, a wee ribbon of road runs around the edge of the park, a conveyer belt of toy cars. Jordan leans and pokes his head to see things. He shoots questions into the air while pointing. The museum, St Giles – all the places we've neither of us been to since school trips. I put the big brother out of my head and decide to just enjoy this. Maybe I need this cold and these views. I can feel it doing me good, though I've still got the ache from last night, the pictures coming and going in my head.

Frank. The Regent. Rab – oh god, Rab. I bundle into myself at the memory of me half-heartedly ransacking the flat then tidying up again, suddenly sober, thinking better of it. Did I do all that? Was that me?

One thing I do remember. When I finally slunk out the door I left my key.

I finally left my key.

'You remember the big fish tanks in the museum?'

Jordan, breaking into my thoughts.

'Those goldfish freaked me out a bit.'

'I used to spend a long time sitting there looking at them, just thinking.'

His sideys are a mix of brown and grey and gold. Weird I've never actually seen him in daylight before. He turns to me, grinning, and I see again that kid from biology class. After a while I can't help myself: I reach over and touch the side of his face.

He leans in. 'What a day, though. Look at that view.'

'Place has its moments.'

We sit there hunched over and silent. Anyone watching would think we were boyfriends.

'So, how come you missed your train?'

'This morning, first thing, I was still planning on leaving. But... I can't remember if it was saying goodbye to my brother, or when I couldn't get my mother on the phone, and I really had this need, this *need* to speak to her. Or maybe it was earlier than that, I don't know. I can't remember what it was that decided me or even if it's this now, sitting here with you, but I've realised or made my mind up or whatever...' He laughs again. 'Sorry, am I making any sense?'

'Don't really know what you're on about.'

'I mean, I have to go back to London,' he says. 'But maybe I'll be back here again sooner than I thought.'

He gives me the side-eye.

'Sounds good,' I say.

'Really?'

'Yeah, course.'

'Trouble with me is, I just open my mouth and let my belly rumble.'

I'm thinking how little I know him, really. We have that connection, school, all that. And then there's the small matter of all that sex we've had. But then there's all those years in between, a big hole in the middle of the story.

I have an impulse to kiss him, right on the edge of his mouth. I do it, and then wipe at the powdery toothpaste streak I've left there.

He smiles and puts a hand over mine.

'The thing is, I made a fool of myself with someone,' he says. 'A friend. A good friend. But, you know, that's all he was, a... We were never more than friends. And I thought the best thing to do was to... move on.' He sighs. 'I'm tired of running.'

I listen without saying anything, not sure yet where he's going with this. He's got that look he wears sometimes. Like it's all about to kick off under the skin of his face.

'Anyway, I just wanted to tell someone.'

I don't say anything. I'll miss this moment when he's gone.

I can feel him beside me shivering, so finally I tap him to his feet, and we go back the way we came, half walking, half trotting because his knee's giving him gyp, and the way down's harder than the way up.

He asks about my trip, and I tell him I'm looking forward to it, even if the prospect of getting on a flight or a boat to Portrush and the old boy gives me a feeling inside that's like a fright.

It's something, though, a plan.

I'll sit down with him, the old boy, and ask him about his life, and hope that he does the same.

Then home to my friends. Carol, Dan, Luca, Evie. The thought of them, of us all together, well, there's a comfort, like taking your shoes off at the end of a long shift.

'Mate, watch!'

Down in the park a football rushes past my ear, and I'm all the way back again, all the old fear of having a ball hit me in the head. It bounces on the ground next to us, quite hard. Jordan lumbers ahead and boots the ball back to a crowd of boys, right on target. Pretty impressive in a way.

'Thanks, mister!'

As soon as the boys have gone he bends to rub his leg.

I drop back a little and watch his shoulders swing up and down as he walks, the way his hands gangle at his sides. I slow down, then slow some more. I could just drop away, disappear myself, let him go off into his life without me.

He turns before he gets out of sight, searching with his eyes. 'David?'

'Maybe I'll go a longer trip,' I say, catching up with him. 'After I've seen my dad. Spain. Galicia, you know – I could go a tour. See some of my mum's part of the world.'

Did I say all of that out loud? I can feel my face heating.

'And then, well, I haven't been to London since I was a kid…'

He stops walking, and in the silence I think he's going to tell me off for getting carried away.

'Please come,' he says. 'I'll take you round all the galleries.'

We walk on. Round past parliament and the palace again. We stop to take a look at a girl in full paint and Dracula cloak, hiding behind a pillar, smoking like her life depends on it, waiting for the ghost tour to arrive. She sees us nebbing and takes a wee fluttering bow, and we both laugh, though there's something quite scary about her pasty face in the afternoon light.

We get to Abbeyhill, climbing the road where it runs under the viaduct. Jordan stops to take a look at the student digs; he has to crane his neck to see all the way up. It's funny, seeing these changes through his eyes.

Passing the Regent at the top of the hill I huddle into my jacket. Last night, the visit to Rab's, my trip to the house, it might have happened to a different person. That's the grimmest part. It was like an out-of-body experience.

'I haven't been in the Regent for years,' Jordan says, and the way he says it, I worry he's going to suggest a pint, but instead he launches into a story about some legendary night out when he was younger. A bunch of neds wandered in, there was a fight, some poor boy got glassed and the police came.

All this way across town I've felt strange – I mean, like I can't quite catch my breath, the need to say something growing in my chest, my insides tight at the thought of getting the words up and out.

Only I'm not sure what to say, how I'll put it. It's not the kind of thing you can just drop into the conversation.

Beside me Jordan's grin comes and goes with each bump of the road, as his voice keeps on about all the stuff he remembers about this part of town, all the things that were there when he was last here and the things that weren't.

Down on Easter Road we stop at the window of the Twelve Triangles.

'Would you look at all this?'

Cakes are like sculptures. I follow him inside, relieved for a break from the schlepping about. I ask for a coffee while Jordan has a tin of ginger beer: sooks it all the way to the dregs. Cuts up his Black Forest into bits. He looks into his ginger beer tin like it's a telescope, gives his funny side-laugh, and gets all bashful when he sees how little progress I've made with my strawberry tart.

'Not really a massive fan of sweets,' I say, pushing my leftovers across.

I want to lean myself across the table and say, *I'm not who you think I am.*

It's close to cashing up, so when we go up to pay the counter staff tell us we can have a few pastries on the house. Jordan turns to me, like he needs my permission.

I wait outside while they bag up for him. Through the window I can see him smiling and passing the time of day with the counter staff.

I feel it pounding inside me, this need to share.

Door thuds and he's there beside me, so delighted with his bag of leftovers, like he's won the lottery, and the roar gets louder.

'Jordan…'

'You okay? You look—'

'Knackered, I know.'

'Handsome. I was going to say handsome.'

His face is kind.

'Jordan…'

And then the roar within is overtaken by something else, a surprise rush, weather stampeding up the hill towards us. I flinch back into the doorway, tight as I can get, while Jordan just stands there, holding his spot, happily turning wet. He laughs and gives a shout, tries to pull me under with him.

'Urgh, you're a… fucking lunatic, you.'

We're both laughing. I'm drenched. Jordan's drenched. I'm thinking of yesterday, when I was there screaming into the rain, but without any of this laughter.

We're stamping around in the puddles. Rain fucking everywhere, and even when it lightens, it's a while before I can persuade him to move on.

*

I wasn't expecting today to end like this. Back at the flat, everything between us seems slower. We're not on the clock for once. He doesn't feel the usual need to talk on and on. Not in the hall where we get out of our clothes, or in the shower, where he's content to stand holding me from behind with his head resting against the top of mine. He lays his forehead against the back of my head, so soft it just about knocks me out.

I hold him there for a while, so he can't see the tears slipping down my face.

So clean and so tired when we get into bed, it's like we're newborn. I watch until he's asleep. My head's an all-out sports day of words jumping over each other, trying to get to the front place in the line-up.

I think about shaking him awake. I lie there, unable to get the air all the way to the top of my lungs, and when I'm up to here with it I get the hell up and go through to the living room and dig around. Paper. Pen. There's a load of old bills and missives thrown around the table and the floor – it's all pretty depressing. I rummage around until I find the best-looking envelope.

I stand in my jammy bottoms at the kitchen counter. I have to keep stopping and restarting – it's so long since I've used a pen for anything other than taking down orders. Scrumpled bits of paper gather at my feet, but I keep going, finding a kind of flow, and then the words come faster and better.

The one thing I could do at school was write.

My thoughts keep falling off cliffs in my head. Why am I doing this, anyway? What am I even trying to achieve?

When I'm done I read it over a couple of times, and I'll admit I'm quite proud of what I've written. Fold it into the envelope and write his name. Underline it twice. Smooth over the envelope as much as I can, but it's a shabby parcel. No way of gilding this lily.

At the window I watch this runner weaving a violent zigzag down the middle of the road. A car goes past, and he staggers sideways, blown off course. I get tense, but then he performs this funny parody of a tap dance, which allows the rest of his body to catch up with his legs, restoring his balance for the moment. I feel like cheering.

Tomorrow I will get out my laptop and I will book the tickets to go see my old boy. I'll phone and tell him I'm coming, and I'll make light of his reaction, whatever the hell it is. I'll try to get hold of my pals, tell them I've missed them, rally the team together.

Jordan shifts and grumbles but his eyes stay shut. I stand by the bed for a while with the envelope in my hand. He'll laugh when I hand it over. *What, did I forget my birthday?* Then I'll watch him unfold and read, and I'll see his face change, and that will be a painful moment. And if he lets me, I'll tell him the rest, and it might be a way to something more.

Maybe.

Acknowledgements

Thank you to the brilliant people at Fairlight Books: Greer Claybrook, Sarah Shaw, Beccy Fish, Louise Boland, Amy Blay, Emily Bromell, and, especially, Laura Shanahan, my editor, for gently encouraging me to be clear in my intentions and bold in my execution.

I'm grateful to the writers who have kept me going through a busy couple of years: George Anderson, Sophie Cooke, Kevin MacNeil, Theresa Muñoz, Pippa Goldschmidt, Mary Paulson-Ellis, Daniel Sellers, Zoë Strachan and Louise Welsh. Thanks to everyone at the Scottish Book Trust for years of support, and to Ditte Solgaard Dunn for her exceptional photography.

Thank you always to my friends and family, especially Ryan, Sean, Isaac, Iain, Aileen and my parents, Mary and Bill, and my heartfelt thanks to everyone who has bought, read and recommended my work.

About the Author

Allan Radcliffe was born in Perth, Scotland, and now lives near Edinburgh. His debut novel *The Old Haunts* (2023, Fairlight Books) was shortlisted for Scotland's National Book Awards and for the McKitterick Prize, and was adapted as a BBC Radio 4 Book at Bedtime. His short stories have been published in anthologies including *Out There*, *The Best Gay Short Stories* and *New Writing Scotland*. With an MA from the University of Glasgow, he works as an arts journalist and theatre critic. His writing has won the Allen Wright Award and the Scottish Book Trust New Writers Award.

ALLAN RADCLIFFE
The Old Haunts

Shortlisted for Scotland's National Book Awards and the McKitterick Prize 2024, and adapted as a BBC Radio 4 Book at Bedtime

Recently bereaved Jamie is staying at a rural steading in the heart of Scotland with his actor boyfriend Alex. The sudden loss of both of Jamie's parents hangs like a shadow over the trip. In his grief, Jamie finds himself sifting through bittersweet memories, from his working-class upbringing in Edinburgh to his bohemian twenties in London, with a growing awareness of his sexuality threaded through these formative years. In the present, when Alex is called away to an audition, Jamie can no longer avoid the pull of the past: haunted by an inescapable failure to share his full self with his parents, he must confront his unresolved feelings towards them.

In spare, evocative prose, Allan Radcliffe tells a wistful coming-of-age story and paints a tender portrait of grief in all its complexities.

> '*Equally heart-warming and sorrowful. Each and every sentence has been so elegantly penned… a pleasure to read*'
> —*The Scots Magazine*

> '*Elegant and unshowy, it dazzles with a distinct and irresistible inner luminosity. A stunning, indelible debut*'
> —Kevin Macneil, author of *The Brilliant & Forever*

OLA MUSTAPHA
Other Names, Other Places

Mama, Baba... and Mrs Brown.

Wayward Nessie is caught between cultures: too English for her Tunisian parents, yet not 'white enough' or 'African enough' to fit in with any of the groups at school. Her father is determined to make the family 'respectable', while Mama is lost in nostalgia for the country she left behind. Even Nessie's sister Sherine, who appears to find it easiest to slip between identities, faces struggles of her own.

Then there is the charismatic Mrs Brown, who befriended her parents on their arrival in England. She soon becomes the glue holding the family together, until one day she disappears from their lives as quickly as she arrived.

Years later, struggling with patterns of self-sabotage, Nessie returns home to confront the mysteries of her childhood. Forced to re-examine everything she thought she knew, she begins to wonder: what really happened between her parents and Mrs Brown?

'*A novel of rootlessness and family secrets, which tells its truth with briskness and deftness*'
—Leila Aboulela, author of *River Spirit*